FORGED IN LOVE

NIGHTWOOD CLAN SERIES BOOK 4

HARPER DAKOTA

Warning:
This book contains mature themes and is intended to be read by ages 18+. Contains sex, some curse words, paranormal and magical themes, fated mates, and two men in a loving relationship. Mention of rape of a secondary character; event is not described, only mentioned.

Trademark Acknowledgements:
The author acknowledges the following trademarks and trademark status of these items mentioned in the book, including:
Ticket To Ride
Oban Distillery
The World's End
Oban War & Peace Museum
Oban Chocolate Company
Perle Oban Hotel
Furglars

Cover Design by: Jay Aheer

Editing by: Lori Parks

To my husband. Thank you for helping make my dreams come true.

FORGED IN LOVE

At one hundred and fifty years old, Ian finally had everything he wanted.

Becoming a vampire when he was eighteen, he viewed it as his chance to find his own fated mate, to explore the world, to live and see new things. He has never regretted his choice, finding friends among paranormals and humans. When he finally meets his mate, he's amazed that Fate brought him such a perfect fit. Berkley's handsome, caring, creative. Everything Ian could have wanted in a partner. They settle into their life together, but when a fun outing takes a dangerous turn, will Ian and Berkley be able to save themselves, or will bigotry and hatred win?

PRE-NOTE FROM THE AUTHOR

Thank you for picking my book to read! I hope you enjoy it.

If this is your first time reading one of my books, or it has been a while between reads, here are some helpful things so you don't feel lost.

- There is a character list in the back of the book.

- Mates and members of the Clan can speak telepathically to each other. This type of communication is indicated with a single apostrophe and the words are in italics.

Scottish phrases used:
Mo ghaol (my love)
Mo chridhe (my sweetheart)
Piuthar (sister)
Sgain-dubh (small knife worn tucked into the sock when dressed in traditional kilt)

Scottish accent words used:
Aye (yes)

Bairn (child / son / daughter)
Cannae (can't)
C'mere (come here)
Da' (dad)
Didnae (didn't)
Dinnae (don't)
Hae (have)
Ken (know)
Mam (mom)
Nae (no)
No' (not)
Shite (shit)
Wee (little)
Weel (well)
Ye (you)

PROLOGUE: IAN

I an came up to the house, eager to see who was visiting. He had been checking on the animals in the fields when he'd noticed two strange horses tied up in front of his parents' home. He hadn't known that they had been expecting visitors or he would have rushed through his chores sooner. It was boring on the farm. They had the animals, and he helped his da' in the forge, but they didn't get a lot of visitors. The most exciting time was when they went into town, and even then, it was the same old people every time.

"Mam, Da'. I saw some horses outside. Is someone here?" Ian called out as he skidded into the house.

He found two other adults sitting at their kitchen table. His mother was sitting, clutching a cup of tea, pale as anything. If he believed in hauntings, he would think she had seen a ghost or something. He didn't recognize the man, but the woman looked like a younger version of his mother. She looked vaguely familiar, like he had seen her before.

"Mam. Are ye alright?" Ian asked, concerned, walking to stand behind his parents. He wanted to make his stance clear. He had worn his dirk today since he'd been working out in the fields, but he was hoping he didn't need to use it inside the house. The man was large. Not much taller than Ian's own six-foot-four frame, but he was definitely wider. His muscles were huge, unlike Ian's own leaner build. Ian would bet the man would have no problem with the caber toss in the Highland Games.

"Ian, this is your Aunt Agnes and her…husband Robert."

Ian looked at his aunt as they stood up to shake his hand. He knew his mother was the younger sibling, but this woman looked closer to Ian's age. She had the same dark red, almost auburn, hair and hazel eyes that Ian and his mother had. She stood about the same height as his mother. The man looked about his parents' age though. He did not look Scottish like the rest of them. He had dark hair and eyes that were watching them all closely. He seemed very protective of his wife, almost like he expected Ian's family to hurt her. Which made absolutely no sense to Ian.

"It's nice to meet ye both," Ian said, trying to be polite. There was a weird undercurrent in the room that he didn't understand.

"You've grown so much," Agnes said. "The last time I saw you, you were about eight years old, I think." She looked over to Ian's mother for confirmation and got a single head nod in response.

"Oh. I'm sorry. I dinnae really remember ye," Ian replied awkwardly. Her accent was very faint, he only heard a wee bit of Scottish in her tones. He really wished he knew what had happened before he came in the house. Did they have a fight? Why hadn't he seen her in ten years? "Did ye move away?"

"I did. I met Robert and discovered he was my m—perfect person. We got married and traveled for a couple of years. I came back for visits, but we finally moved away for good when you were eight. Robert has land in England that he needed to tend to. We are thinking of traveling to America for a little while and wanted to make the time to reconnect before we leave." She glanced over at her husband, a pause happening before she stood up. "We are staying at an inn nearby. Would it be alright if we came to visit again tomorrow?"

Ian waited for his parents to respond, but when there was no answer forthcoming, he replied, "Yes, I look forward to getting to know ye again." He walked with them to the front door.

"I think Mam must have been shocked to see ye after all this time. I do look forward to speaking wi' ye again," Ian said, trying to smooth over whatever had happened.

"It does get awfully monotonous around here, doesn't it?" Agnes asked. It wasn't said in a mean way, more of a sympathetic, commiserating way.

"It does. I can only talk to the sheep and cows for so many hours in the day," Ian said, laughing. "Da' has been letting me work on my own in the forge more, but it does get dull at times."

"I remember that well. I was so excited when Robert came into my life. It has been such an adventure, traveling and seeing new things."

"I would like to hear some of your stories," Ian said. He knew there was more to life than just his little town and the other ones close by, but his parents never seemed inclined to venture far from home.

"I would love that," Agnes replied. She had missed so much of their lives and was hoping to have a chance to reconnect. She smiled at Robert as he raised her hand to kiss her palm, trying to cheer her up.

"You are always welcome to stop in and see us, as well," Robert offered. He thought Ian had the same adventurous spirit that Agnes had. He could see the same mischievous gleam in the boy's eyes that was in his mate's. He had been hopeful coming here that she could connect with at least one of her family members. Her parents had since passed on. He didn't have much hope for her sister and her husband though. They seemed a little too set in their ways to accept them. Ian, though, he held promise. He would like to have some more family, Robert mused. He only had his brother and his mate, but they didn't see them very often with their different traveling schedules.

"You may want to check with your parents," Agnes advised. "I do not think Charlotte is very happy with me at the moment and I don't want to cause any fighting between the three of you."

"Did ye have a fight?" Ian asked.

"Of a sort," Agnes replied. She wasn't sure how much to tell him. She had come to offer a different kind of life to her last remaining relative, but it had not gone over well. She certainly didn't want to come between her sister and her only child. "I think it would be best if she addresses it. I don't want to cause more problems." She really didn't. Maybe it had been impetuous to come and think her sister would be open to another way of life. She just hadn't wanted to lose the last of her family.

"Alright," Ian said slowly. He really needed to speak to his parents and find out what had happened.

Agnes moved forward, hugging Ian tightly. Robert shook his hand before helping Agnes mount her horse. "We'll see you tomorrow then," Agnes said, before riding off with Robert right behind her.

Ian took a deep breath and headed inside. His parents were still sitting at the table, talking quietly. The conversation stopped as soon as he came in the room.

"Mam, what happened? Why are ye angry with your sister?"

"She's changed. She's no' the same person I knew before and I dinnae ken that I want her around ye," his mother replied bluntly.

"Was she mean? She didnae seem awful," Ian responded.

"No, she wasn't mean."

"Did she make ye feel bad because she has fancy things?"

"No. But that Lord of hers…"

"Robert? He's a Lord?" Ian asked.

"Yes. He changed her."

"Well, I imagine being wi' someone for so long changes everyone. Ye always tell me that ye hated even the look of blood pudding, but now ye make it for Da'."

"No, he… She's spouting off about fate and things. God controls everything, no' some notion of fate."

Ian sat for a minute. "Well, if she's no' mean and she's no' causing harm, I dinnae see what the problem is."

"She just isn't the same. I dinnae like the changes she has gone through," his mother replied stubbornly.

Ian sighed. He really wanted to get to know his aunt and new uncle. It was dull here and he never quite felt like he fit in. At the very least, he wanted to get to know them and hear their stories. "It's her life, Mam. She clearly still loves ye and wants ye in her life. I think that says a lot about her. I'm going to go check on the animals again. Do ye need help for dinner?" he asked, standing by the door. He had rushed the last few chores once he saw the horses and he wanted to make sure he hadn't missed anything in his haste.

"See if we have any ripe vegetables, please," Ian's da' finally spoke up. "Can ye close up the workshop as well? I'm going to help your mam in here."

The next day, Agnes and Robert came around lunchtime. Ian and Agnes did most of the talking. His mother would try to change the subject anytime traveling came up. Ian thought she knew that he wanted to leave their small village and see more of the world. She had always been too fearful to go far. At eighteen, he was ready to spread his wings a bit.

"Why are ye going to America?" Ian asked.

"It's time," Robert responded. "My property in England has a caretaker and we'll come back to check on it from time to time, but America has so many opportunities right now, new things to see. Maybe one day you could come visit us. We can send our address when we find a new home," he offered.

"Absolutely not!" Ian's mother shouted.

"Mam!" Ian was taken aback. "It's just an idea. I would love to see something new. I would be safe wi' family."

"No, ye would no'," she replied mulishly.

"What is going on between ye? They haven't been aggressive or mean. So she changed her beliefs a wee bit; I dinnae understand why you're being like this," Ian stated. He knew his parents were set in their ways, but this seemed extreme.

"It's no' natural."

"Char—" Agnes began.

"Aggie, shut up. Ye come here after years wi' nothing but some letters, wanting to change our whole life. Ye speak of fate but no' God. You're trying to take my son."

"I have done nothing of the sort," Agnes replied indignantly. "We offered to have him visit us, that is it. Nothing more. He has the same sense of adventure that I have, Charlotte. He will be crushed here if he stays and never sees anything beyond a fifty-mile radius of this village. The offer I made ye is no' the same one I made him. I wouldn't do that without speaking to ye."

Ian sat at the table, watching the sisters shout at each other. Aunt Agnes's accent was stronger now, the Scottish coming through as she got upset.

"Psh," Ian's mom scoffed. "It doesn't matter. He doesn't need to leave to find something to enjoy. There are plenty of girls in town, he can find a wife to create a life with. He can create things wi' James in the forge. It is a fine life."

"Yes, it is a fine life. One that ye chose. He may want

something different. I'm no' evil for finding a new path in life. I still go to church, I help others when I can. I'm really no' that different from who I hae always been," Agnes protested, her voice hurt, the brogue strong now.

"And if he goes to America, he could be hurt or even killed on the crossing. He could find some girl to marry over there, and I would never see him again. Never see any grand-children. He's my only child and he should stay here."

"If that happened, you could come see him or he could travel back to see ye! For goodness sakes, Charlotte, ye are no' chained to this village. There is a whole world out there to explore!"

Ian watched as the sisters continued to argue. His da' and Robert were staying out of it.

"Mam. I'm no' going to get married," Ian said quietly, his heart racing.

"Ye just haven't met the right one yet. When the village has its Highland Games, you'll hae a chance to meet some of the girls from neighboring towns."

Ian shook his head. He never really wanted to bring this up to his parents, hoping he could just live his life alone. He noticed Robert staring at him. He just knew that Robert had somehow already guessed his secret, but the man simply gave him a single nod.

"Mam. I'm no' getting married," Ian repeated.

"Ye'll find a nice girl. Ye're a nice-looking young lad and hae useful skills," his da' added helpfully, awkwardly patting Ian on the back. Ian supposed he was trying to be supportive.

"You're no' listening to me," Ian said firmly. "It doesn't matter if I visit them or stay here. Ye won't lose me to some lass in America. I am no' getting married. I dinnae want a lass for a wife." He rushed his words, emphasizing the word lass, before running out of the house. That was as close as he was going to get to telling his parents that he didn't look at girls that way.

He grabbed his horse, throwing on a bridle before jumping on its back and rushing off. It wasn't the first time he had ridden bareback, and he didn't want to take the time to put on the saddle. He headed to open land and let his horse have its head. Racing across the land, he tried to let the wind rushing by him take away his thoughts and problems as well. A few minutes later, Ian brought his horse to a stop at a rocky outcropping. It was a good place to sit and think. The sun was still high, making it seem warm on this spring day. He didn't want to cause upset in the family, but he knew he wouldn't be happy if he allowed his parents to push him into marrying a girl someday. Girls were not appealing to him at all. It was the boys that held his attention, their muscles making his cock stir. Lord, it had been quite a few years ago now since he had realized that he was mesmerized by the rippling, sweaty muscles of the men doing the caber toss and the stone-put, not the lasses wandering around in their best outfits. He had known what his parents would say, so he had kept it to himself until now.

He lay down on top of the rocks, nestled into a smooth spot that had been worn down through the years, an arm under his head. His chores were done, so he could stay here a bit until it got darker. Then his aunt and uncle would have gone, and they wouldn't be witness to any more fighting. It would be amazing to see America though, wouldn't it? Ian wondered if he might still be able to go one day. Agnes was right; he did want to see more than just his small village and the surrounding ones. The warm rock and the light breeze lulled Ian into relaxing, his eyes sliding shut.

Ian was startled out of sleep. He had no idea what woke him, but what really sent his heart pounding was the feel of the smooth thin body curled up at the base of his throat. Breathing as shallowly as possible, he cracked one eye open, hoping he was wrong. He could see just a bit of the tail trailing down over his shoulder, the black zig-zag pattern unmistakable. It was spring and he had been on the rocks in full sun. He should have been more careful, he internally yelled at himself. Adders usually avoided people and their bites weren't terribly toxic, but he also wasn't sure if that held as true when bit in the face or neck. Ian lay there for several minutes, panicking. He did his best not to move, not even muscle twitches, and to keep his breaths slow and shallow. How did he get this snake off his neck without scaring it and getting bit? He couldn't reach his dirk without moving his arm and shoulder, which could startle the snake.

Suddenly he felt a breeze rush by him, and the snake was gone from his skin. Ian kept his body still, but his eyes tracked a blur of movement. He watched as the blur stopped, suddenly looking like a person, the snake flying off into the distance. Ian blinked and Robert was suddenly right next to him.

"Did it bite you? Are you alright?" Robert asked, grasping Ian's head gently and turning it side to side, looking for bites. "Aggie is going to smack me if you got hurt. I was supposed to bring you back home safely."

"I'm fine. It dinnae get me. How did ye...what...ye..." Ian sat up, his words trailing off.

Robert sighed and sat by him on the rocks. "We weren't going to tell you unless Charlotte gave us permission, but I guess it's hard to hide the secret now. Your aunt and I are... different. I have some extra abilities, like being faster than a human, but I'm still the same person I ever was. So is your aunt."

"Faster than a human? Are ye no' human?" Ian asked incredulously.

"Not exactly," Robert winced. "I was born human, but I changed many years ago. I'm a hundred and sixteen years old."

"That's no' possible," Ian interjected. "Ye look around my parents' age, no' some decrepit old man."

Robert paused, his eyes not quite focused on Ian. He huffed out a laugh. "Addie loves that. She's never going to let me forget it."

"What is really going on?" Ian asked softly. "I'm no' stupid. I ken there is something that everyone is keeping from me."

"Kind of like the secret you've been keeping to yourself?" Robert inquired back, his voice soft, sympathetic, not at all harsh like Ian would expect.

Ian flew off the rock, ready to run.

"Ian. It's alright. I promise. My brother didn't fancy girls growing up. He was still my best friend. I didn't care. He was out late one night and got caught kissing another bloke. Some arseholes at the tavern stumbled out at the wrong moment and saw him. The other man had run off and George was outnumbered. They ended up beating him so badly that he almost died. Luckily for George, another man ended up walking by and fought off his attackers. Matthew arrived just in time to stop George from dying, but it was very close. To save him, he had to turn my brother. After that day, they went everywhere together. Matthew seemed like the perfect partner for George. When I was forty, I noticed my brother wasn't aging and asked him what was going on. He gave me a choice and I chose to turn as well. I traveled with him and Matthew, his mate, for a while before going off on my own. I eventually met your aunt. She is my mate, my perfect partner. Aggie chose to become like me and spend the rest of our lives together."

"Mate, like a friend? Turn into what?" Ian asked. He was glad he was finally getting somewhere with having some answers.

"I need you to listen and not run off. You can ask me any questions you want, as long as you promise to be a little open-minded. If you can agree to that, I will tell you," Robert replied, looking at Ian, a serious look on his face.

"Yes, I can do that."

Robert nodded, acknowledging their agreement. "There is a whole other world of creatures that live alongside us. Those of us not human are, as a group, called paranormals. There's a large range of species; werewolves, other animal shifters, Fae, witches, vampires. The majority of us do not fit the evil lore depictions of us, but there are always some who are just bad people. For the most part, we try to live our lives hidden from humans, or at least without drawing attention to ourselves. We want the same things; to find love and hopefully our fated mate, the one person meant for us, to have a home and friends. My life changed a little bit when I turned, but I'm still the same person I was when I was human. I will simply live much longer now and be a little harder to kill."

Ian listened, forcing his feet to stay planted in one place, doing his best to keep his promise to listen. "You're a vampire then? Ye were very fast when ye grabbed the snake."

"Yes. Your aunt is as well. Each paranormal species has their own characteristics, and then some people are gifted with an extra ability. While all vampires are faster than a human, I am very fast."

"Are ye immortal? What's a mate? How did ye change? Did ye have to give up your soul? How are ye out in the sunlight? I saw ye drinking tea at the house, can ye eat food?"

"No, we're not immortal, we just live for a much longer time. There are very few species that are immortal. A fated mate is the one person that is our perfect match, our soul mate, if you will. We recognize them when we meet them; it depends on the paranormal, but ways that I have heard of recognizing a mate is by touch, smell, or dreams. If the mate is human, they have a few options. They can remain human and not complete the bond, they can complete the mate bond and remain human but gain our lifespan, or they can choose to join their mate in becoming a paranormal. If their mate is a different type of paranormal, I believe their lifespans will match to the longest one.

"Vampires live to about two thousand years or so. We can be killed, it's just harder. To turn, you must be bitten by a vampire who is intentionally trying to turn you. If they were simply feeding, you would not be turned. Yes, we must drink blood. We do not need to kill someone to feed, we can close the bite marks and if we didn't take too much, they will be fine. There are of course some people who were evil to start with or who later chose to become evil, but becoming a vampire doesn't make you a bad person if you were not such to begin with. There can be a bit of blood lust in the beginning that can cause problems if no one is there to guide a new vampire. We can attend any type of church; I was never very religious, but I attend church with your aunt. We can eat regular foods. The sunlight doesn't bother us unless we are already severely injured. There are certain poisons that I've heard can kill us, and there is always death by burning, being stabbed through the heart, and decapitation," Robert stated. "It's too hard for a body to heal if it is reduced to ashes, the heart is destroyed, or your head is missing. We still have a heartbeat, our heart and lungs still function, so if the heart is destroyed, the body cannot function."

"Why are ye telling me all of this?" Ian asked, confused. He would think they would want to keep what could kill them a secret.

"I want you to feel comfortable around us. Your aunt really missed her family, and we were hoping to be able to stay in touch. Your parents do not seem as open to the idea as we had hoped, which I know makes Aggie sad; but if she could still have you, she would be happy."

"Why are ye moving to America then? Do my parents ken ye are vampires? Is that why they're upset?"

"Yes. We told them what we were. Aggie began staying away when she wasn't showing her real age and tried to maintain contact through letters. When you have hundreds or thousands of years ahead of you, it can be easy to forget to do things on a human timetable, so the letters started becoming more infrequent. When she realized you would be eighteen, she was aghast that so much time had passed, and she wanted to reconnect.

"Neither of us has much family. I have my brother and his mate. Aggie has your family. She offered to turn your parents, but your mother was horrified. I half expected her to have a priest here when we came back. Not that it would have done anything. I could bathe in holy water, live in a church, walk around completely bare during the height of the sun if I wanted to. Those things don't affect us. In fact, I met a vampire priest one time. Nice guy. Aggie promised not to tell you about us since your mother wouldn't let us meet you otherwise.

"We're moving to America for a couple of reasons. It will be exciting to see new things. The main reason, however, is that people start to notice when you don't age. We get around it for a little while by leaving the area and coming back as our own heir. There are a few witches around that specialize in magical spells to help keep our properties in our possession. They make the deeds and wills link to our bloodlines and the names will automatically change when we create a new identity. I have some very long-lived humans that live near my estate and who work or worked for me that are starting to question why I look exactly like my 'father,' so I thought I would take a hundred years or so and live somewhere else. The magic will keep the estate in my possession and the land and title will simply pass down to myself as my own heir. If that makes any sense," Robert tried to explain.

"I think so," Ian replied. "What is involved wi' being turned?"

Robert looked at him for a moment. Ian started to worry that he wouldn't answer.

"Before I tell you how, you need to know that it's not something that can be undone, other than death. It's a different kind of life, one that has a lot of possibilities, but there are drawbacks as well. You generally can't live in one area for your whole life without people noticing that you do not age. There are a few ways around that like living in a remote area, certain spells over your property, but in general it is safer for you not to live in an area for too long. Other downsides include superstitious people that may attack you, and while you are hardier, you can still be injured or killed. Other paranormals may attack you; remember, there are good and evil people no matter the species. Some people have a harder time adjusting to their new reality than others, even those that chose it. If you don't have paranormal friends or family, it can be lonely. Humans die so quickly that it can be depressing to form bonds and have them die in just a few short years. We also keep our existence as secret as possible, so making long-term relationships with humans is difficult. The secrecy is to protect both paranormals and humans," Robert added, almost as a warning.

"Why are ye telling me then?" Ian questioned.

Robert sighed before answering. "I'm pretty confident that your parents will not turn. I don't want Aggie to lose what's left of her family. If she could keep in contact with you, I think it would make her happy. However, I'm also not convinced your mother would let those letters reach you. If you knew to expect them, you could look for them. Agnes would smack me if she were here, but I also wanted you to know that turning is a possibility for you. Maybe your parents decide to turn, maybe later in your life you decide you want it, or maybe you aren't even interested, but I wanted you to have the option. You remind me a lot of your aunt, the same drive to explore the world. It would be safer for you to travel if you were a paranormal. Certain areas are more open to men who desire other men, but there are places where you would be beaten to death if you were caught. I wish it wasn't so, but at this moment in time, that is the way of it. If you were turned, you would be able to defend yourself better and survive the bigots. Paranormals, as a species, tend to be more open about different types of relationships. We live so long that most of us simply want to find happiness. I have seen Fate pair the same sex, opposite sex, and even multiple partners together."

"If I decided to turn, would ye stay and teach me?"

"Yes. There's no real deadline of when we need to go to America. Everything has been set up; it would simply be a matter of us booking our travel. We are far enough from my estate that no one should recognize me, so we could stay here to help you adjust. It's a quick process to start the turn. I would bite you with the intent of turning you. You would have to drink some of my blood as well. You would sleep for one to four days while your body finished changing. Some new vampires have a great thirst, some adjust easier. Some have a new gift right away, some develop one later, some only possess the normal vampire traits of increased speed, sight, hearing, healing, and strength."

Ian sat down again, mulling over everything Robert had told him. He was certainly tempted to join them, both in travel and in becoming a vampire. He loved his parents, but they were fearful of change and the unknown. He did not see them ever traveling far from their home. He yearned to leave and see new things. His village was small and conservative. He would never find a partner if he stayed here, nor did he think the village would welcome him having a male partner. Although he had been resigned to living and dying alone, the small hope that he could find someone to love had always been there. If he became a vampire, he would be able to search for his mate. And it would be a little easier since he would know them by smell. Well, easier than simply guessing as a human. He would still have to find them somewhere out in the entire world.

The sun was beginning to set, which meant that Ian needed to gather his horse and head back home. He hadn't brought a lantern with him.

"Aggie said to bring you home. Your parents are convinced I ate you," Robert said sardonically.

"That's ridiculous. Let's head back so I can talk to them. I'm interested in your offer though. I know there is something more out there for me," Ian replied.

Ian mounted his horse and took off at a gallop. Robert kept pace with him, not even looking winded or tired. When they arrived at the house, his parents were frantically waiting for him in the yard.

"I told you Ian was fine, Charlotte," Agnes said, exasperated.

Ian took his horse to the barn and got him settled before confronting his parents.

"Robert saved me and then we got to talking," Ian told his mam.

"Saved ye from what?" she replied, disbelief in her tone.

"I fell asleep on the rocks and an adder decided to fall asleep on me. It was on my neck, and I didn't want to startle it. Robert was fast and grabbed it off me. We need to talk," Ian said as he headed into the house.

He sat at the table, waiting for the others to come in. He was trying to gather his thoughts before he spoke.

"Robert told me what he and Aunt Agnes are. I saw how fast he moved when he grabbed the snake and rushed it away from me. I ken why you hae been acting strangely toward them, but they hae no' done anything wrong. I want to become like them. I want to travel, to see things besides our village and the neighboring ones. I want to meet new people. Maybe one day, I can find a partner of my own. It won't be a girl, that will never be an option for me," Ian stated plainly.

"Ye can see things wi' no' becoming such a creature," his mam protested.

"They're still people, Mam," Ian scolded. He grabbed the cross off the wall, the one he knew his parents had had blessed by the priest. "Here, Aunt Agnes. Can ye hold this for me?"

Agnes smiled at him, her eyes twinkling with humor. "Of course, nephew." She reached out and held the crucifix for a moment before placing the end on top of Robert's hand. It wasn't that heavy; it was to prove a point that it didn't affect either one of them.

"They're no' evil, Mam. They're just a wee bit different now. Robert dinnae hae to save me, but he did," Ian said.

"Oh, no. I most assuredly did. Aggie would have killed me if I let anything happen to you," Robert protested.

"I want to turn. I want the chance to find my own mate, who will be a man. If that is something that ye cannae accept, I will make sure ye have help on the farm and then I will leave with Aunt and Uncle. Either way, I will be turning and eventually leaving to travel the world. The part that is up to ye is if I stay here for a while before traveling and then coming back to visit or leaving now." Ian sat back in his chair, half convinced his parents would ask him to leave for his desire. His aunt grabbed his hand, squeezing it in support. Robert gave him a head nod.

"I dinnae ken where this is coming from," his mam protested. "Did ye just hide it from us?"

Ian knew she was speaking about not wanting a wife. He nodded but kept silent. His stomach was churning and he didn't think he could speak without the possibility of vomiting.

His mam started crying, not sobbing, more that there were tears leaking from her eyes. "Ye are my only bairn, Ian. I dinnae understand this, but I am no' going to lose ye. If your mind is made up, then we'll support ye."

In the end, Robert and Agnes stayed for almost four months. The first month was to teach Ian and his parents about the different paranormals and to set up the magic around the property. When his parents decided to join the paranormal family, Robert brought in a witch to help with their land title. Because his parents would never leave, they added a little extra bit of magic to help them blend in with the townspeople better. Ian wasn't sure what the magic entailed, but Robert assured him it would enable his parents to stay in one place for the rest of their lives. Robert told him that since his parents were pretty self-sufficient, it would be easier for his parents to stay in one place; whereas Robert's house and land had a lot of employees who were always around and noticed if he didn't age.

After that first month, Robert turned Ian. His mother still didn't trust Robert, so Agnes had turned his parents. The rest of their time was spent teaching them how to be vampires and helping them adjust. His parents were wary of biting people, so Robert purchased extra cows and a few pigs for them to have as secondary food sources. It wouldn't be as good as human blood, but it would be enough to keep them fed and healthy. They would just need to breed the animals or buy more to keep their food source plentiful. Once they were settled in their new lives, Robert and Agnes left for America after having Ian promise he would keep in touch and would come visit one day. Ian had chosen to stay on the farm for a while to make sure his parents had really adjusted and that they would be alright on their own.

He spent some time traveling around Europe, exploring the different countries. He felt a little guilty that his parents had changed their lives so much because of him, and he wanted to be close enough that he could get to them quickly and help if needed. During those years, Ian studied with different blacksmiths, learning new techniques and methods. He also started working with leather, finding it was a good creative balance. Not to mention it was easier to make and sell while he was traveling. As the years passed, he was grateful for the new technology that allowed him to get letters faster, then telegraphs, and then phone calls to his aunt and uncle. He kept in contact with them frequently, but it wasn't until his last trip home to Scotland that he felt an unrelenting urge to finally visit them in America. A few phone calls and a plane ticket later, he was on his way across the ocean. He had a feeling his life was about to change, bringing him everything he ever wanted.

PROLOGUE: BERKLEY

Berkley sat on the stool, contemplating how he had ended up here. His magic, of course, was to blame. He had been born in England, growing up in a smallish Fae village, though it had been a while since he called it home. He had walked away from the village a hundred years ago trying to find his spot in the world. The village he grew up in was small enough that he knew everyone there. As a young child, he played with the few other children and helped his parents around their home. During the summer, he played in the fields, chased after butterflies during the day and hunted glowworms at night. Children were rare among the Fae, so he had only a few people his age in the village. He enjoyed living there and didn't think anything was missing from his life. It wasn't until puberty came that everything seemed to change.

Fae discovered their fated mates through sight or touch. As everyone he grew up with came of age, the village hosted a formal gathering where there was dancing and food. The Fae who recently became old enough to find mates were put on display. Berkley stood in front of the entire village with the few others around his age. He was dressed in his nicest clothes, his long silvery hair combed and neatly braided.

It had been a nice warm night; the moon was bright and torches and lanterns lit the area. The field had been the meeting place for the village for as long as Berkley's family had lived there, which was to say for hundreds and hundreds of years. The stage had been rebuilt several times, expanding as the village grew. Or at least that was what his parents had told him. Berkley remembered being directed to his place on the stage, his stomach churning with nerves. He hated being the center of attention, but he had stood there, trying to keep still, hoping that the evening would reveal his fated mate. The elders had given a long-winded speech about mates, traditions of the village including the practice of taking a life partner, and the duty of making children to help the village flourish. Berkley and the small group standing on the stage were informed that if you did not find your fated mate, you had a *duty* to eventually find a life partner when you were ready to settle down. Life partners, Berkley knew, were simply someone you decided that you were compatible with, and you lived together as partners. Some couples were together hundreds of years; however, unlike fated mates, they could decide to later part ways or even add another person or persons to their relationship. Berkley didn't want to spend his life alone, but he quickly dismissed choosing a life partner as an option. First, he worried that he wouldn't find someone that he could connect with enough to want to have a sexual experience with. So far, he had none of the urges that he had heard his friends and older siblings talk about. Second, what if he took a life partner and one day their fated mate came along? Berkley would be cast aside and alone once again. Even if he was the one that found his fated, he would hate to hurt someone else's feelings. He had no desire to be put in that kind of position, even though the chances of a mate stumbling upon him were almost zero. The village was rather remote, and it had additional warding that kept strangers and non-Fae from entering. Berkley had looked over the crowd, feeling uneasy as he thought back to the only other mate-finding gathering that he had attended as a small child, and realizing that there had not been any fated couples resulting from it. It was mandatory for all to attend, so if you didn't find your mate at the gathering, they were either not in the village or were not of age yet. It was rare that someone left the village to search out their fated, most being content to remain in the village and find a life partner.

Berkley had shoved his concern down. He could still remember standing there, feeling more like an object than a person. The elders had walked by each of them and listed their name, age, interests and hobbies, and other details. He felt like he was a sheep they were looking to put up for auction. When the elders were finally done speaking, the singles in the village had walked by to inspect them closer, which he had thought was ridiculous. It wasn't like they hadn't known him his whole life. Of course, there was a chance that he just hadn't been in close proximity to someone since he had come of mating age. The village was small, but he could go a month or more without seeing certain people. As the line ended, the music began to signal the time for dancing. The dances were fast-paced, the ones where you switched partners often. The goal had been to give everyone a chance to see and touch the new adults. Children had their own little party off to the side of the field, watched over by the few fated pairings in their village. Everyone else had been required to dance. What seemed like hours passed as Berkley put his best face forward, dancing with seemingly every adult not related to him. When the elders called an end to the music, no one had found a fated match. Berkley was disap-pointed, but he was also relieved that the night would be ending. It had been a lot of people interaction, and he just wanted to have a nice cup of tea, maybe read a book before he went to bed. His stomach had been in knots the entire night and he simply wanted a chance to relax.

The elders stood on the stage, sending all underaged children home. Berkley waited for them to say goodnight to the adults as well. Instead, he was shocked to discover was that as soon as the children were gone, the evening devolved into one big sex party. The elders went on to encourage them to explore their sexual side, nothing was off-limits. Well, other than relatives. There was no restriction on the gender, age, or number of participants. Growing up, he hadn't been oblivious; he knew sex was common and that partners frequently changed. He saw it among his older brother and sister. They had not found their fated mates at their own gathering and while they had not chosen a life partner yet, they never seemed lacking for a sexual playmate. He had no problems with others taking care of their urges, as long as everyone consented. It just wasn't something he was interested in. The problem was him; he could find someone attractive but the desire to bed them due to their looks wasn't there. He tried to leave, having no desire to participate. However, the elders had ordered him to stay, telling him that it was his duty to become sexually active with anyone he desired in the hopes that he would create children and/or find someone to eventually choose as a life partner. Berkley didn't see either of those happening tonight; paranormals had very low birth rates no matter how much sex one had, and he thought he wanted more than just sex, he wanted a friendship, some sort of connection with someone.

Berkley tried staying on the fringes, hoping he would be ignored. When an old friend came up to him, the top of her dress halfway unbuttoned, her breasts full and almost falling out, her hand reaching for his cock, he had swallowed hard. He hadn't wanted to offend her or make a scene, so he tried. He really did. His cock twitched, but that was it. He didn't feel any desire from the kissing, no rush of heat from touching her breasts. He didn't get fully hard even when a muscular male body came up behind him, an erect cock pressing against his back. He had ended up slipping out from between them and running back to his parents' home, ignoring any other calls for him to play. It had been quiet when he arrived at the house, his siblings still at the party, his parents were shut in their room, although he could hear grunting noises coming from behind the door. The next day he realized just how much one evening could change his place in the village; the others he used to go to school and play games with now viewed him as strange for not having participated the night before. They were all too busy embracing their new sexual freedom and didn't want to spend time with someone who preferred to read or work instead of having sex. He lost the few friends that he had, unless he counted his relatives.

It was fine, he had told himself. He dove into learning new things and helping his parents. He told himself that having his family was all he needed. They were great; he had a relatively large one with a brother and a sister, which was almost unheard of among the Fae. He had some aunts, uncles, and cousins as well. He created his pottery and helped in his parents' shop. It was all fine, just fine, not exciting, not extremely fulfilling, but fine. One day, his soul started telling him to leave, that what he was looking for was not there, to go, to search, to find something more. So, he went. His parents had been visibly upset at his leaving, giving him a pat on the back from his father and a quick hug from his mother. It was more than he had expected; the Fae were not known for outbursts of emotion and physical touch or affection outside of sex was extremely limited. It seemed to work for everyone else in the village, but it felt lacking to him. Or maybe he was just broken in some way.

He traveled around England, eventually expanding his search to surrounding countries for thirty years, before his magic urged him to make another big move, to take a voyage across the ocean. There was something there calling to him. He resisted for a while, unsure of taking such a huge step, but his magic persisted, poking at him until he booked passage. He stopped to see his family before he left, letting them know that he was leaving for America, that he didn't know when or if he would be back. He stayed in his old room for a night, saying his goodbyes. His mother had told him to write her when he arrived. There was a new postal delivery route that passed nearby, and she had made the village a post box so that they could keep current and receive mail as well. It sat outside the warded limits of the village but was still within a reasonable walking distance. That had been thirty years ago.

Which brought him back to now. He had been traveling this country with no sign of what he was looking for. He had met new people, made a few casual friends, learned some new things, but nothing that seemed important enough to have made such a long journey. He was currently sitting at the bar in a tavern in some random small town because his magic told him to stop here. He was really wishing that the drunks behind him would either leave or pass out. He had been planning on spending the night in one of the tavern's lodging rooms, but these gentlemen were quickly changing his mind. Before they had arrived, it had been relatively quiet and he had enjoyed a nice meal. The barmaid had been very flirtatious in the beginning, but when he didn't return her advances, she quickly left him alone. While her breasts were certainly plentiful and bouncy, he had no real desire to pursue any relations with her. Nor did he feel inclined to step out back with the handsome bartender who made an offer earlier in the evening. He appreciated the beauty in both genders, but he still rarely felt the need to pursue the attraction he might feel. He hoped that one day his mate would come and fill that void. The barmaid gave him one last flirtatious offer, probably because her other options for company were the drunkards behind him.

"What's the matter, pretty boy? Too much woman for you to handle?" drunkard number one slurred as she walked away, having been gently turned down again.

Berkley finished his drink and slid the money across the wooden surface. He needed to leave before the insults turned into a physical fight. He was fit, but there were five inebriated idiots sitting at that table. He was loath to use his magic in the tavern with so many humans around.

The bartender came over to take the money. "Tony is an asshole. You might want to sneak out the back to avoid him," he said quietly.

Berkley nodded his thanks and slipped away toward the bathroom. He kept walking, heading out the back door. He made it down the road a couple of blocks before he heard voices behind him.

"Hey! We was talkin' to you," drunkard number two shouted.

Berkley kept walking but took his hands out of his pockets. He wanted to be ready if they tried to attack. He could fight if he needed to, but he was vastly outnumbered and there were still too many houses nearby to safely use his magic unnoticed. You never knew when someone was going to look out their window, and he had no doubt that someone would be with how loud these idiots were being. Berkley held no hope that anyone would help him though; he was, after all, just passing through and these men lived here, or at least nearby.

"Didja hear 'im, pretty boy?" There was drunkard number three, he thought sourly.

He sighed. Was it too much to ask for a simple night of a meal, a drink, and a bed to sleep in? Why couldn't people mind their own business? He stayed to himself most of the time, trying not to draw any attention. He just wanted to be left alone.

A rock hit his back as drunkard number four got his shot in. "We don't need freaks like you in town," the man shouted.

Berkley had no idea what these men's problem was. He hadn't looked at them, hadn't spoken to them. He hadn't taken the barmaid or the bartender up on their offers, so he wasn't infringing on their hunting ground, so to speak.

Another rock hit the back of his head and he started to walk faster. That one had stung, and he wondered if it had managed to cut him a little. If he could get off the main street, away from prying eyes, he would use his magic. These men were probably too drunk to remember anything clearly tomorrow anyway. There was still one man unaccounted for, unless he stayed behind, he thought hopefully.

Shite, he thought to himself as the fifth man stepped out between some houses in front of him.

"Where ya' goin'? We ain't done talkin' yet," he stated. He seemed a little more sober than his friends. Still an arsehole though.

"I'm just trying to get home, if you will let me pass," Berkley said calmly. If he didn't escalate things, maybe they would leave him be. He was not terribly optimistic about that happening.

"Nah. I don't think so. See, we don't want your kind here. Best to teach ya a lesson so you don't come back."

Berkley rolled his eyes. His magic gathered inside him, ready if he needed it. "What kind would that be?"

"Pretty little freaks. It ain't natural for a man to look like you."

Well, it's not like he could control his looks, Berkley thought to himself snarkily. He wouldn't be able to hold his own against five other men in a simple physical altercation. He was going to need to use his magic and could only hope no one was looking out their windows when he did. Maybe he could simply make them all fall asleep, and no one would get hurt that way. They needed to sleep off the alcohol anyway.

"What's going on?" a deep voice growled behind him.

Werewolf, his magic whispered.

"Nothing you need to be concerned about. Just move on," the fifth man replied.

There was a hint of nerves in his voice, causing Berkley to turn around to see exactly who had scared him. There were two men standing there, both a little taller than his own five-foot-nine-inch frame. The werewolf was blond with green eyes, his body trim but with broad shoulders and large muscles. The vampire standing next to him had black hair and piercing bright blue eyes. He was also tall, but more of a lean muscle build. Berkley could see why the other men were scared; the newcomers both had a presence that was commanding and lethal.

"No, I beg to differ. It seems like you're harassing our friend, so that means it does concern us," the vampire replied. "Would you like to continue your conversation now that we're here, or would you prefer to leave?" There was a definite emphasis on the leave.

"We'll just be off," drunkard number four muttered as he tried to drag away number five.

Berkley watched until they were far enough away. "My thanks," he nodded to the other paranormals. His magic was pushing him toward them, *friends* it kept telling him.

"Anytime. My name's Rolf," the vampire said, extending his hand in greeting.

"I'm Sam," the werewolf added.

"Berkley," he replied, giving them his name.

"We're on our way home if you would like to join us? There's still safety in numbers, even for us. It's a tiny town and my house is small so it might be cramped, but we should all fit. It's a couple of days' journey away, but it's a safe place," Rolf offered.

Berkley used his magic to take a close look at their auras. Friends, it still insisted. It had been a long time since he had friends outside of his family. "I would love to," he replied.

As they walked along, his magic kept a lookout for the troublemakers, but they didn't show up again. Berkley had been traveling alone for a long time, so he mostly listened to his companions' conversation. He spoke up if they talked to him directly, but his peopling skills were a bit rusty. It had still been a pleasant journey and he felt more comfortable speaking up by the time they arrived at Rolf's house. It was indeed small, but they made it work. They dismantled Sam's bed frame to use the wood to make a set of bunkbeds along one of the walls. Rolf had the remaining single-frame bed. There was a kitchen and a fireplace to keep them warm in the winter.

It wasn't much, but it was home. Sometimes all of them would be there, sometimes one or two of them would leave to explore. They always came back though, knowing that they had a safe place and a family of sorts to come home to. They were all individuals far from their families, or in Sam's case, his parents had passed away and he had been an only child. Over time, Rolf added on to the land and they helped clear a larger section for a small farm and for a bigger house when all three decided to stay put for a while. They helped look over the small town they called home and as people grew to accept them, the townspeople helped look after them as well.

Looking back, it still amazed him that one thing could so drastically change your life. One night lost him all his friends in the village. One meeting would give him lifelong friends and finally a place to belong and call home. The only thing missing was his mate.

1

I an grabbed his laptop and headed into the library. He needed to call his aunt and uncle and catch them up with everything that had happened recently. There had been a lot of change and upheaval that had occurred in just a couple months. All those years ago, he had been determined to turn so that he could find his forever person. It had taken years of traveling, honing his crafts, moving to a new country, finding his then-human best friend, and later being called to Shaye's home to help fight off an evil vampire with illusions of world domination, but he now had a mate, his business, his best friend/chosen sister, and a larger family made of their friendships. This was everything his younger self could have wanted. Berkley had made the remark before that it was amazing how one incident could change your life so completely. Ian couldn't help but agree; if his aunt hadn't come to visit, he wouldn't know of vampires. If he hadn't decided to turn, he would have died long before he could have met Berkley. If he hadn't moved to America to start a new life, he wouldn't have met Shaye, his best friend. If he hadn't been friends with Shaye and come to help, he wouldn't have met Berkley. He also wouldn't be part of this amazing new family.

He pulled up the video call and waited for someone to answer. His leg bounced as he listened to the ring tone.

"Nephew! How are you?" his uncle Robert asked cheerfully.

"I'm good. Is Aunt Aggie there too?" Ian asked.

"Let me find her. You can come with me," Robert said laughingly as he started walking. "I think she's outside painting."

"How's that going? Is she still liking it?" Ian asked. His aunt had just begun exploring the creative side of painting when he had lived with them. She was pretty good, he thought.

"She is. She has a showing at one of the local galleries next week," Robert replied, pride in his voice.

"You'll have to send me some pictures. I'm glad she's still enjoying it. How's Clara?" Ian asked after his cousin. She had been born in the United States, about eighteen or so years after his aunt and uncle had arrived. They got along well, but she had the same restless bug that he and his aunt did. She hadn't been living at home when Ian had come to stay, so they mostly connected over the phone and texting. It was nice when they were able to meet in person though.

"She's great. She decided to try out for a Broadway play and she was offered a part. Lord knows that she has a broad enough background to do pretty much anything," Robert replied, fond exasperation in his voice.

Ian grinned, knowing his cousin had taken classes in everything from cooking to ballet to voice to piano to Krav Maga. "She's in New York then? She had mentioned heading that way, but I wasn't sure if she ended up there or got distracted by something else."

"No, she's there for now. They've been practicing quite a bit. We'll see how long it lasts. Hopefully she'll at least finish out the season and not leave them in a lurch. Luckily for them, it's a touring show. I think it will keep her more entertained if she's changing cities fairly frequently," Robert replied.

Clara was a bit of a free spirit. She bounced from one thing to another, never settling for long. "I'll have to see if I can't catch a showing nearby. It'd be great to see her. I have someone for her to meet too," Ian added, working his way into why he had called.

"Oh?" Robert said, raising an eyebrow. "Hold on, let me force Aggie away from her brushes. Ag, put that down and come here! Ian's on the phone," he shouted, although it was a bit muffled so he must have put his hand over the microphone.

He could pick up the faint murmur of a response, and the sounds of brushes being set down and swished in a liquid.

His aunt popped up next to his uncle in the screen, a smear of blue paint on her forehead. "Oh, good lord, Robert. Why didn't you tell me I had paint on my forehead?" Aggie asked.

Ian laughed as his uncle just grinned.

"There was a stupid fly that wouldn't leave me alone," Aggie explained. "I must have painted myself when I brushed it away." She reached for something off-screen and started scrubbing at her skin. The paint had dried though and wasn't coming off easily. She snorted in disgust and flung the rag away. "Whatever. You've seen me worse," she said. "Now, tell me everything."

"Ye might want to take a seat," Ian warned before jumping into his story.

"So...ye remember Shaye?" he asked, thinking it would be better to start at the beginning rather than bounce around in the storyline.

"Yes. She's such a sweet girl. She still sends us Christmas

cards every year. Did you finally stop being a twat and catch up with her?" Aggie asked.

Ian nodded. When he had gotten to the age where he should have shown some signs of aging, or even scarring from some of the accidents that he had that she knew about, he had started slowly pulling away from his friend. Which had just about killed him, emotionally. In general, it wasn't looked too favorably upon letting humans know about the paranormal world. Aggie had encouraged him to just tell her, but he had been too worried about the harm it might do instead. Shaye already had been dealing with years of having emotionally abusive and neglectful parents, plus the side effects of her own healing gift; he didn't want to thrust her into the occasionally dangerous world of paranormals by revealing what he was. He had started using phone calls or texts more than video calls. When he did take a video call, he would often flip the screen around to show what his newest project was instead of focusing on his face. He started taking a lot more traveling gigs to consume his time. Of course, Fate had laughed at him and given her a vampire mate.

"I did, although no' for the reasons you're thinking of. I had been staying busy wi' traveling Renaissance festivals. I was worried about dragging her into the paranormal world when she was already having such a hard time with her gift. Turns out, Fate is funny. Shaye has a vampire mate and she turned back at the beginning of November."

"That's amazing! Have you met her mate yet?" Robert asked, sitting down and pulling Aggie into his lap.

"Yes…this is the part where ye cannot yell until I'm done, okay, Aggie?" Ian asked.

She mimed zipping her lips.

"So, her mother-in-law is great. Emma's like the house mam to all of us. Rolf, Shaye's mate, is a great guy. He has a big house in Tennessee that we've all moved into. We officially became a Clan at Thanksgiving, although it's no' all vampires. Long story short, Rolf's dad was a fuckwit. He, uh, forcibly made Rolf; Emma and he were no' mates. When Rolf was old enough, his da' came back, turned Rolf without asking, but laid it on real thick afterwards saying how he wanted to be part of his life and such. Rolf traveled a bit with his da' but started noticing things that weren't right. He eventually left and tried to get back to his mam," Ian rambled before taking a breath. He looked at his uncle, seeing by his widened eyes that he had put some of the story together.

"His da' didn't like that, trying to kill his mam. Rolf got there in time to turn her. Rolf moved to the US and met Shaye. His da' had tried killing him for not joining with him, but Shaye found Rolf and saved him using her healing. After the second attempt to kill Rolf, they came up with a plan with some of Rolf's friends and Tess, our friend from college. Shaye wanted to be turned so that she could hold her own better in a fight against Vlad," Ian added. He almost laughed as his uncle hurriedly put his hand over his aunt's mouth, stopping her from yelling at him. "Yes, it's that Vlad. Well, was that Vlad. Shaye and Rolf killed him in the battle."

Ian cleared his throat as he saw his aunt's eyes narrow at him. He was going to be in for a lecture when this was over. "They asked me if I could help, so I went. They hae such a great group of friends here, we're more like a family. Doc and Emma are the oldest, although I think Doc is the only one who is actually the oldest in terms of age. Emma just seems more like a mam; she was turned in her mid-forties and of course, is an actual mam to Rolf. Tess, ye know from college, and her mate Sam. He's a werewolf, runs the local brewery and restaurant. Gawain is a falcon shifter, and he discovered his mate recently, Merri. She's a witch and is Tess's sister. And then there's Berkley," he added, unable to stop the grin from spreading across his face. "He's Fae and has his own pottery shop in town. He's amazing. I can't wait for ye to meet him."

"He's your mate?" Robert asked.

Ian nodded. "He should be home soon, and I'll hae you meet him. I wanted a chance to get yelled at without him here," he added cheekily.

"Is there anything else you need to tell us before I let your aunt loose?" Robert asked, amusement in his voice.

"No' really. I'm going to start my own physical shop here, either sharing in Berkley's shop or the shop next door may go up for sale soon and I would buy that. Rolf is giving us a place to put in a workshop for both Berkley and me on the Clan grounds. We haven't had a chance to finalize a plan yet with the attack on Sam and Tess…" he trailed off. "Um, yeah. So, Vlad had a follower that was trying to take over his spot and attacked them on their way home from visiting her family. Luckily the spell wasn't able to finish killing him, and once they got home, we were able to form a Clan bond and help send energy through Shaye to destroy the spell. Uh… yeah, I think that's it…helping kill Vlad, meeting my mate, signing Clan paperwork, forming an old-school blood link with the Clan to save Sam… Yup, that's it," Ian said cheerfully.

Robert nodded. "That's quite a bit in just what, two months? I'm going to let her go now," he warned, slowly taking his hand away from his aunt's mouth.

"Ian! I can't believe you didn't tell us this before now. Does your mother know?" Aggie demanded.

He winced, shaking his head. "We're going to go see them soon, maybe January or February. I'll tell her then. I'm safe; anyway, it would just cause her to worry until she could see me."

"We would have helped," Aggie said.

"I didn't think of it," Ian admitted, glad she couldn't reach through the phone to smack him.

"Next time you go up against a delusional, speciesist, egomaniac psycho, please let us know ahead of time so we can help," she added.

"I'm hoping we won't come across any others," Ian admitted. "But I promise."

"Did you say you formed a blood link?" Robert asked. When Ian nodded, he let out a sigh. "I didn't think those were even done any longer. I've only heard stories from Matthew."

"The death spell on Sam was spelled against witch magic, so Tess and her family couldn't heal him. Shaye had to rely on using only her healing powers. Normally Tess and Berkley would send their magic through Shaye to help, but this time Tess couldn't because of the way the spell had been cast. Once Shaye saw that the mate bond was helping hold it back, she thought we could try using the Clan bond in the same way. Rolf tried linking us all using his telepathy so that we could see and fight the spell but couldn't connect that many people at once. The blood link was the only way we could think of to save Sam in time," Ian explained. "We were already a Clan, a family. It wasn't a hard step to take with the blood link."

Aggie cleared her throat, blinking. "Well, I'm glad you finally found your place," she said. She really was happy for her nephew. To find your mate was a such a gift, and to be able to find a group of friends who you counted among your family was another blessing.

"Did you get in any trouble after the Vlad incident?" Robert asked. Having that big of a disturbance should have caught the attention of someone.

"No. Our local Sheriff is also the Warden for the area. Rolf had spoken with him beforehand, and he helped with the cleanup. Well, he did a lot of the paperwork afterwards, the dragon really helped with cleaning up."

"There was a dragon?" Aggie exclaimed. Goodness, her nephew was meeting all kinds of new people.

"Yup. He was huge too. I'm glad he was on our side. Once the Sheriff was done documenting and taking pictures for the records, the dragon burned the bodies. It made it so much easier keeping what had happened from the town finding out."

Ian tilted his head, his mate bond letting him know that Berkley was close. "Berkley's almost home. Did ye want to meet him?"

"What kind of question is that?" his aunt scoffed. "Of course, I want to meet him!"

A minute later, he heard the library door open and felt a kiss on his head as Berkley came to sit beside him.

"Aunt Agnes and Uncle Robert, this is my mate Berkley. Berkley, Aggie and Robert," Ian said.

"Hi, it's really nice to meet you," Berkley said, threading his fingers through Ian's. He was a little nervous about meeting Ian's family. "I wanted to say thank you as well, for turning Ian and giving him the chance to be himself. I never would have met him otherwise."

"It's lovely to meet you as well," Aggie replied, smiling. "I'm so happy Ian found his mate."

Berkley leaned against Ian, relaxing as his aunt and uncle spoke to them. They felt like his family too by the time they got off the call.

"They seem nice," Berkley said, resting his head on Ian's shoulder. "Did they yell at you like you thought they would?"

"Eh, not as bad as I thought it would be," Ian admitted. "They loved ye," he added, giving Berkley a kiss. "Ye know what I just thought of?"

"Hm?"

"Rolf is locked in his office working, Emma's down at the clinic, Gawain never leaves his room, and the rest are still in town working. Want to head upstairs?" Ian asked, blinking flirtatiously.

"To help you get something out of your eye?" Berkley asked dryly.

"Shut up! I was going for flirty," Ian laughed, shoving at Berkley's shoulder before standing up.

"Don't try that one again," Berkley advised, keeping his face straight. He stood, grabbing his mate around the waist and pulling him close. "I would love to go upstairs with you, even if you don't have an eyelash in your eye," he said with a grin.

"Brat. Let's go then. I want us naked on the bed, and me inside ye. Now," Ian said, dragging Berkley out of the room.

They stumbled up the stairs, hands groping and stopping occasionally for kisses. Berkley reached out and fumbled for the doorknob, not willing to let go of Ian's lips so that he could see. He finally got the door open and they fell inside, Ian kicking it shut behind them. As soon as he heard the click, Ian lifted Berkley, hands under his thighs, moving to hold him pinned against the door. Their cocks lined up perfectly and Ian rutted against him, the friction causing them both to moan. Berkley's fingers tangled in Ian's shorter red hair, pulling his head back so that he could lick his way down his neck, sucking a love mark near his collar bone.

Ian took a step away from the door, walking them over to the bed and letting Berkley slide down to sit on the edge of the mattress before stepping in closer between his legs. Berkley grabbed the bottom of Ian's shirt, drawing it over his head, exposing his hard nipples. He reached out, lightly tugging on the barbells, causing Ian to hiss, his hips involuntarily thrusting toward Berkley.

"Get naked, mate," Ian demanded, ripping his own pants off, before leaning down to toss Berkley's shoes across the room. He was watching Ber's face, his cheeks flushed, the purple-blue of his eyes almost lost to his blown pupils. He loved seeing an aroused Berkley.

Berkley lifted his hips off the bed and Ian pulled the pants off, throwing them somewhere behind him. Berkley licked his lips, looking at his man's toned body, it was slim, lean, but held such hard compact muscles. He didn't have much body hair, just a faint little trail leading to his cock, the trimmed red pubic hair a shade darker than his head, a smattering of freckles scattered about, his hazel eyes watching Berkley hungrily. Ian's cock was already hard, a drop of precum glistening on the tip. Berkley reached out, scooping it up with his thumb before licking it off.

Ian groaned, watching Berkley's mouth. He leaned down for a kiss, tasting the faintest hint of himself, before pulling Berkley's shirt off as well. His position gave Berkley the perfect angle to lean in and lick Ian's nipples. "Fuck, love. That feels good, bite please," Ian grunted. Ian watched as Berkley pulled his lips back, gripping the nipple between his front teeth, and bit down.

"Shite, just like that," Ian said, holding Berkley's head to his chest. He reached down and grasped Berkley's dick loosely in his hand. His mate was hard, his shaft silky smooth but hard as a rock. Berkley was a wee bit thicker than he was, Ian's fingers almost not touching as he stroked him. It was a beautiful cock, long, and thick enough that Ian was always delightfully sore after they had sex. Normally Ian topped, but sometimes Berkley wanted to change it up, which Ian had no problem with. He would take his mate any way he could get him. Ian pulled Berkley's head away, gently pushing him back on the bed before leaning to the side to grab the lube from the nightstand.

Stepping back between Berkley's legs, he coated his fingers with the lube, gently sliding a finger across Berkley's hole, watching as it clenched for him. Ian swirled his finger around the furled circle before slowly pushing a finger in. Gently thrusting, he slowly worked at opening Berkley up for him, leaning down to kiss him before adding a second finger. Berkley was so tight, his muscles clenching around his fingers before relaxing enough that Ian could move. He gently stretched him, alternating between thrusting and scissoring his fingers.

"Harder," Berkley demanded, his hips chasing after each withdraw.

Ian let his hand move a little harder, a little faster, his fingers curling to press against the prostate, Berkley arching and groaning as he found the magic spot. Ian watched as Berkley writhed on the bed, the sounds pouring out of his mouth letting him know just how much he was enjoying it.

"In me, now, Ian," Berkley demanded, his legs coming up to wrap around Ian's waist, pulling him closer.

Ian slicked a little more lube on his dick, knowing that Berkley was just barely stretched enough to take Ian's shaft. He pressed his tip against Berkley, feeling a little bit of resistance as he breached Berkley's body. His breath caught at how tight his mate was, the heat that engulfed him making Ian clench his teeth, pausing to allow both of them to adjust. He wanted his lover to come first, and he fought down his own rising pleasure. No other bed partner could ever compare to the feeling of being inside his mate. When Berkley relaxed enough for him to slide the rest of the way in, and he was no longer in danger of shooting off too soon, Ian grabbed Berkley's hips, pulling him closer, tilting his hips up a little bit, just enough that his penis rubbed against Berkley's prostate with each thrust. Ian kept his thrusts slow and measured, concentrating on his lover's pleasure.

"Oh god, Ian. Kiss me," Berkley demanded, desperate to feel his love coming inside him. His own cock was moments away from exploding, even untouched. He grabbed Ian's hair, pulling him down to kiss, his tongue plunging in to claim Ian's mouth just like his dick was claiming Berkley's body. He opened their telepathic mate bond all the way, loving the rush of sensation as Ian did the same thing. It was a sensory feed-back loop that soon had them both gasping and shaking with the need to come, seconds from reaching their climax.

Berkley's hips rose to meet each of Ian's thrusts. *'Bite,'* Berkley pleaded, turning his head to expose his mating mark. The sensation of Ian biting and drinking from Berkley was guaranteed to send him over the edge.

Ian licked the spot before sliding his teeth through the skin, his mouth filling with Berkley's blood. Reaching down, he stroked Berkley's shaft as he drank. He groaned as his lover's body clenched around him, his cum coating Ian's hand and dripping onto Berkley's stomach. Ian's hips lost their measured rhythm, pounding into Berkley's body, the orgasm ripping from him. Licking the bite closed, he gently pulled out, watching as his cum started to leak out. Berkley let his legs fall to the bed, a blissed-out look on his face. Ian ran to the bathroom, grabbing a washcloth to clean Berkley off, finding him still laid out on the bed, content smile on his face. Ian wiped Berkley down before pulling him farther up on the bed and dragging a blanket over them.

'Okay?' he asked, lying on his side propped up on his elbow. He wanted to make sure he hadn't taken too much.

'Mhm,' Berkley replied, his voice content but sleepy. *'Snuggle nap,'* he declared, pulling Ian down to lie with him.

He could nap, Ian thought, his eyes closing as he held Berkley close.

2

I an held Berkley's hand, giving it a kiss as they waited near the living room. Everyone was helping move Doc's things into Emma's room at the Clan house today. He was glad they were finally all going to be together under one roof.

"Everyone ready?" Shaye said from the front door. "Rolf told them to make sure they have clothes on before we get there," she added, laughing at her now red-faced mate.

Ian burst out laughing. Emma and Doc were definitely still in the honeymoon stage of being newly mated. Ian could completely understand not wanting to walk in on your mother doing various adult activities, but he was still going to find a way to tease Rolf about it sometime today.

Berkley grinned at him, his unique purple-blue colored eyes laughing. *'Will we have to watch ourselves at your parents' house as well?'* he asked over their telepathic link.

Ian shook his head. *'No. I'm not even sure how they had me, to be honest. I dinnae ken that I've seen them kiss more than a handful of times,'* he replied. *'Ye know, we should find time to visit Aunt Aggie and Uncle Robert sometime as well. They'd love to meet ye in person.'*

'We can probably do a long weekend away, try to fit it in before

spring really hits. The tourist season will start as soon as it warms up for longer than a couple of days. Alternatively, I'm sure Rolf wouldn't mind if they came here for a visit as well. There's the small hotel in town, my old apartment above the shop, although we've kind of filled it with storage, or maybe they could stay here. There are some bedrooms still open,' Berkley suggested. He would love to meet Aggie and Robert in person. They had a great time talking on the phone and seemed like they would be a blast to hang out with.

'That's no' a bad idea,' Ian said. *'I'm sure they would love to see Shaye again too. She was over at our house a lot during high school.'*

'I need to set up a call with my family as well,' Berkley mused. *'It's been a long time since I've seen them in person, but I don't think we'll have time to visit when we're seeing your family. The village is a bit out of the way and some of my family have really spread out now.'*

Ian looked at Berkley, a question on his face. His partner never really talked about his family much; Ian hadn't met any of them yet, not even over the phone. He wasn't getting any strong negative vibes from Berkley either, so he wasn't sure what the deal was. Now wasn't the time to get into it though, he thought, as they loaded into the cars to drive down to Doc's. Maybe he could talk to Berkley tonight and figure out what was going on. Despite all their talks, Ian still couldn't nail down Berkley's family dynamic. He had been alone, traveling in the US, until he met Rolf and Sam. There had been no mention of family visits.

'We'll figure something out,' Ian replied.

"Rolf, can ye stop at the bakery before we get to Doc's?" Ian asked as they reached the gate at the end of the driveway.

"Sure," Rolf replied.

"Thanks. I haven't had breakfast yet and I'm guessing they haven't had time to eat either," Ian teased.

"I will smack you," Rolf threatened.

Shaye laughed at them. "Ian, stop teasing my mate. Or do I need to remind you of the time we walked into your parents'…er, aunt and uncle's house and caught them?"

Ian gagged. Nope, he did not need a reminder of walking into the kitchen to find his aunt sitting on the counter with her legs around his uncle's waist. Luckily the only thing he really saw was his uncle's naked arse and back. "I'll stop. Don't ruin my appetite," he pleaded. "They have the best donuts and I'm hungry."

Berkley shook his head, laughing. "I don't think anything can ruin your appetite. You eat more than anyone I know."

Ian shrugged. "I think it's from being turned or maybe having the extra speed. I wasn't like this when I was human."

Shaye looked back at him. "I always thought that was just what teenage boys did. You always hear about their appetites. Although you weren't human when I met you, you never really did slow down either. We used to have to go grocery shopping a couple times a week when we shared an apartment in college," she told Berkley.

They pulled into the bakery's parking lot and Ian jumped out, his stomach now growling. Walking in, he stared at the display case. Everything looked so good, and he felt his hunger ramp up. He heard the bell over the door ding as the rest of the group came inside.

"Good morning, Ian! What can I get you this morning?" Mary asked as she came out of the kitchen in the back.

"I'm going big today, Mary. We're taking breakfast down to Doc's. He's finally moving his stuff into Emma's place. I think we're going to get two dozen donuts, and some muffins and pastries," Ian replied, still browsing the glass displays. There were easily a dozen different types of donuts with a mix of filled and plain, glazed and iced, with a variety of toppings. The blueberry and lemon muffins looked delicious, topped with the sugar sprinkles catching the light. Oh! The bear claws looked really good too, lots of almond slices and icing drizzle. Of course, they needed some lemon bars for Emma and Doc, he thought, remembering that they loved the lemon meringue pies Mary made.

He looked up as he caught a whiff of a bear claw.

"Eat this before you lick the case." Mary laughed. "I can hear your stomach growling from here."

Ian felt his cheeks heat as he blushed in embarrassment. "Thank ye, Mary. I hae no' eaten yet this morning."

Berkley came up beside him and wrapped an arm around his waist, kissing him on the cheek. He needed to start carrying granola bars with him, Berkley thought to himself. There had been too many times lately that he caught Ian forgetting to grab something as soon as he woke up. Maybe he could talk to Doc and get some ideas for protein bars. Berkley had a cousin with an extremely fast metabolism who had accidentally made himself extremely sick by not eating on a set schedule. He should start keeping more food at the shop as well, since Ian was frequently there.

Ian leaned against Berkley while he nibbled on the pecan bar. Mary was assembling the boxes, giving him time to eat. Although he wanted to savor the hint of cinnamon with the sweetness of the icing and crunch of the almond slices, he was so hungry that the pastry was gone in a few bites. Ian made sure to order at least one of everyone's favorite donuts and another dozen pastries and muffins. They may have cleared out a good portion of the breakfast stock this morning. It only took them a minute or so to finish driving down to Doc's clinic. Rolf knocked, waiting for a brief moment before Doc opened the door. It looked like he had gotten dressed in a hurry, Ian snickered to himself. Shaye looked over at him, her eyebrow quirked, daring him to say something. Ian mimed zipping his lips. She rolled her eyes at him, bumping him gently with her shoulder as they walked into the house.

'Thank you, Ian,' Shaye said privately over the Clan link. *'Rolf would have been pouty if he had to think about his mom*

having sex. Good lord, I had no idea the man could be so put out. It's not like it isn't a natural, extremely common thing, especially with mates. He's happy his mom has Doc, but I think he'd rather pretend they don't do anything,' she added, laughing.

'I guess I can understand that,' Ian replied. He certainly never wanted to see his parents or his aunt and uncle like that ever again. Walking back into the kitchen, he placed the boxes down on the small table and countertops, opening the lids so people could grab what they wanted. The front room had been filled with boxes and he didn't want to be in the way once they started moving items.

Emma walked into the kitchen, her hair still wet from the shower. Man, he wanted to tease so bad, but she was like their house mom, and he respected her too much to embarrass her.

"What all are we bringing back to the Clan house?" Ian asked, grabbing another donut.

"The boxes in the front room, which are mostly kitchen and my clothes. I have some medical supplies I wanted to bring to restock the house as well. I was wondering if I could use one of the rooms as an office? The times you guys have been hurt, we have treated at the house, so I thought it would be good to have a room there. I have a lot of books to bring. I have protections here, but I would feel better if they were at the Clan house. There's better protection and almost always someone there," Doc explained.

"That's a good idea," Rolf responded. "There's a small room in the tower that is open on the second floor. The basement has space, or the left side of the house has a few open rooms. On the backside of the house, on the main floor, there is my office and what I keep meaning to make into a theater room. In the front of the house, main floor, we have a pretty big space as well; I just have some knickknack type of things in there now, but those are easily moved. I should probably clean those out anyway; I don't even remember what is in there…"

"Rolf?" Shaye nudged him when he seemed to trail off for a moment.

"Sorry, I went down a rabbit hole of what should be done in the basement. I was thinking I need to convert the bedroom into bunkbeds so we can all fit. It's a panic room slash storm shelter. I may need to get rid of the exercise room down there and expand the storm shelter area, so we aren't so cramped if we ever need to use it. I want to get more shelves and organize the storage area so everyone can have their own space. Anyway, back to what we were talking about, Doc's office."

"I think putting it on the main floor makes sense, that way we don't have to carry anyone up the stairs if we have any more injuries. I think I would prefer it to be in the back of the house though, if that's possible," Doc replied.

"Shouldn't be a problem. I've had that space cleared out for a theater but never actually got started. I'll call in some contractors that I know and have them come look at the space. Feel free to tell them what you want where, or make a list or layout so it's what you need. They can work on the theater room when they're done with that. I think we would have lots of fun having a movie room," Rolf added.

"Thank you. I would feel better having the books and supplies there. I can just store them in our room for now until the construction is done," Doc said.

With everyone helping, it didn't take long to load up the cars. They drove caravan-style back to the house and everyone helped unload. The clinic house wasn't huge, so Gawain and Merri had stayed behind but were helping unpack now.

"How many boxes of books do you have, Doc?" Ian asked, his arms stacked high with boxes. He could tell they were fully packed too.

"A few." Doc laughed.

When the last of the boxes were stored away, Shaye ordered pizza for lunch. Everyone sat around, eating and talking. Ian probably ate a whole pizza just by himself, but he felt full finally and leaned back against the chair, laying his head on Berkley's shoulder. After everyone had finished eating, Rolf looked around the kitchen.

"What do you think of having a celebratory run since everyone is now moved in? Non-runners could walk or just hang out outside?" Rolf suggested.

Doc looked over at Emma, a questioning look on his face. She shrugged in response.

"I would love to run with you, but I have to tell you about my animal first," Doc said. "Berkley, is there a way to hide my animal from everyone but the Clan? I know it seems silly, but once I shift, you'll understand. I have not shifted outside in such a long time, but I would love to run with you," he added longingly.

Berkley took a long look at Doc, trying to figure how strong the spell would need to be before holding out his hand. "Give me your pendant and I can modify it." He held it cupped between his hands, whispering a concealment and protection spell, as well as a modification spell. When he was finished a bright light flashed signaling that the spell took. Handing it back, he said, "It will hide your shifted form and scent from everyone but us. It will also change shape to accommodate your size and is spelled to not fall off." His own magic was excited, and Berkley had a feeling Doc was about to surprise them all.

Doc slipped the pendant back on. After taking a deep breath, he raised Emma's hand to his lips, pressing a quick kiss there before taking a step back from everyone.

"It's better if I'm outside. I don't want to accidently break anything in the house."

Ian looked at Berkley as they followed Doc outside, quirking an eyebrow at Berkley, silently asking if he knew what was going on. Berkley gave him a tiny headshake in response. It looked like everyone but Emma was in the dark. Their family stood together on the patio as Doc walked out onto the grass a good distance away from them, before stopping, facing them, and closed his eyes.

There was a collective gasp and then complete silence once Doc's animal finally stood in front of them. Ian was taken aback. He never would have guessed that Doc was hiding such a big secret, although it made sense that he had. Holy crap, the man was an alicorn. Ian had no idea those were even real. He just assumed they had all died out with only the myths remaining. He certainly had never met one, much less heard of anyone else encountering one. Doc's animal side was gorgeous. He was also huge. The large horse body was a gleaming white, so bright it almost glowed. His wings were coated with matching white feathers, their wingspan impressive. Of course, they probably had to be rather large to get him up in the air. And then there was the large unicorn horn.

Thank goodness Berkley had been able to modify Doc's pendant. He could only imagine the greed of hunters trying to find such a rare paranormal if they knew he existed. Everyone just stood there, not sure if they should move or not. Doc snorted and opened his eyes, looking over at Gawain. Ian turned to see what Doc was looking at. Gawain had the most ridiculous face on. Ian wasn't even sure what that expression meant, but Gawain was certainly struck silent for a moment.

"Um...you're...what...how are...when did..." Gawain couldn't complete his sentences, just trailing off after each start.

Shaye stepped forward. "Can I give you a hug?" she asked quietly, her hand outstretched for Doc's animal form to scent. Of course, his little sister would be the first one to step forward to greet him. She knew what it was like to be outcast for being born differently and not meeting the expectations of your family and wouldn't want Doc to feel like they didn't accept him.

Doc's large head moved down to nuzzle her carefully. The giggle Shaye let out when his soft muzzle tickled her hand broke the paralysis of everyone else.

"Thank you for sharing this with us, Doc," Rolf said as he came over. "We'll keep it safe," he promised. Everyone nodded; Doc was family.

They all took a turn greeting Doc's animal side, letting him catch their scent. When Doc had greeted everyone, Sam ran around the side of the house to change into his wolf. Gawain was lucky enough that he didn't have to take his clothes off before changing forms, and the rest of them had human bodies. Shaye, Tess, and Merri were going to stay back and enjoy the outdoor fireplace, but Emma said she would run with the group for a little bit. Ian thought it was a nice thing to do for her mate.

The evening was perfect for running and they went for a few miles before taking a loop that crossed near the backyard again. Emma stopped, saying she was going to hang out with the girls over their Clan link. Doc ran back to nuzzle Emma before racing off to catch up with the group. When they came to a clearing in the woods, Doc spread his wings and rose into the air. Ian jolted as Berkley grabbed him and yanked him over. He had almost run into a tree because he had been watching Doc instead of where he was going. *'Thank ye, babe. I was distracted watching Doc. That certainly is something isn't it? I never thought I'd see an alicorn, I didn't even think they existed anymore.'* They continued their run through the woods, Sam's wolf sniffing out small animals, Gawain and Doc flying overhead, for about ten more minutes before someone spoke.

'I need to head back,' Doc said over the Clan link. *'It's been too long since I've done this, sorry. I'll have to get my stamina back up,'* he apologized before heading back toward the house.

Rolf slowed to a stop and looked at the rest of them. "Do you guys want to head back too? I'm sure Gawain is about to explode if he has to keep his questions inside any longer," he teased, looking at the branch Gawain was perched on overhead. Gawain just flicked a wing at Rolf, but he didn't disagree.

"That's fine with us," Berkley replied. It had been a nice run, but they would be able to do it again. He smiled as Gawain screeched an agreement and flew off. Sam just shook his head and started chasing him back.

"Want to race home?" Ian asked Rolf.

"I'm pretty sure you'll kick my ass in a race since you have, you know, incredible speed as your gift," Rolf replied sarcastically. "I'm just a slow normal-speed vampire," he added with a grin.

"I'll give Berkley a piggyback ride to make it more even," Ian cajoled. He had a huge grin on his face though, which kind of ruined the effect he was going for.

Rolf shook his head, his lips twitching as he fought his own smile. Berkley knew his friend was quite aware that he would still lose, but he also knew that Rolf was going to give in and let Ian have some fun. "Sure," Rolf said.

"Don't I get a say?" Berkley asked, straight-faced. He did love to tease his mate a little bit.

"Nope. Hop up or I'll carry you over my shoulder," Ian threatened, as he turned around and braced his legs for Berkley to climb up on his back.

Berkley jumped up, his arms and legs holding on firmly. Ian gave his butt a pat before holding him under his thighs. "Ready, set… Go!" Ian shouted. He let Rolf get a few seconds head start, but they still passed him easily. They had already caught up to Gawain as he landed in the backyard, Sam had veered off to the side to grab his clothes. Doc was standing there waiting.

"Okay. I have questions," Gawain said as soon as he was

human. "Alicorns are real? Seriously? How many of you are there? What about unicorns? Do you know any? How old are you? Where did you come from? Why do you shift with your clothes on?"

"Slow down and breathe, Gawain," Doc instructed. "Let's go inside to finish the conversation; I could use another drink." It looked like he had a large empty bowl nearby. He must have had some water in his animal form before changing back.

Ian and Berkley followed their family inside and grabbed a seat on the couch. Doc sat on the loveseat but seemed to be waiting. A few minutes later Emma and Shaye came out with drinks and some snacks.

"Alright, Gawain. Let me start answering some of your questions. Yes, I am real. Yes, I am an alicorn. As far as I know, I may be the only one. I haven't met any others. I find that most flight-based shifters can shift with their clothes on. I am not sure why it seems to be only the flying ones that have that ability.

"Originally my people were from Greece but moved here before I was born. I can speak Greek, as that was the language that was used the most around our tribe. We left because hunters had grown in number, and we were constantly looking over our shoulders and having to hide our animal side." Doc paused, taking a breath.

"Tribe? What type of shifters were your parents?" Gawain asked.

Doc smiled down at Emma as she reached over and held his hand. "They were unicorns. They came over to this land before Erikson made it here. I'm not sure why I shifted differently than everyone else, but the tribe was not pleased. I was kicked out as soon as I was considered an adult. One of the elders, a healer, took me under her wing from the time I shifted until I was made to leave. She taught me about healing and helped me learn what we could about my beast.

There is not a lot of information readily available about the rarer shifters. I am still trying to learn about my animal side."

"What kind of hunters?" Rolf asked, concerned.

Ian knew that running into hunters was never a pleasant experience. He had heard stories from other paranormals, including Rolf and Berkley, about their run-ins. Ian had luckily never had much trouble with hunters himself. He was honestly amazed that it was still a thing people did. As much as the world had become more accepting, he guessed there were always going to be arseholes. Most paranormals just wanted to live their lives, it was the idiots like Vlad who caused problems for the rest of them. He wondered if the hunters knew more normal paranormals if their actions would change to only hunting down the bad of the bunch. Probably not, people could always find a way to justify their actions, no matter the species.

"Because we were unicorns, it was both paranormal and human hunters. Humans wanted the horns for magic and supposed healing abilities, paranormals wanted us for the same thing. Our horns aren't a source of magic though. A lot of unicorns have some sort of healing ability, so if it was a paranormal hunter, you may not be killed, only captured, and enslaved to keep them healthy. Supposedly several of our tribe had been killed or taken, thus the move across the ocean to try to find freedom. However, once more people started coming over, the rumors returned, and we were hunted again. We moved a lot, at least until the tribe started producing several foals and we settled down in one spot. Shifting was extremely restricted, most of it was behind walls or inside a large structure."

"Where was it?" Gawain asked eagerly.

"Near Montana. You're on the right track; although, the last time I was there, there wasn't much of any buildings left," Doc cautioned. "It didn't look like they were attacked, more that they had moved on or died out. I never saw anyone I knew from the tribe again. They were very much isolationists, so it wouldn't surprise me if the tribe ended due to lack of new members."

"How old are you?" Berkley asked quietly. He always had a feeling that Doc was older than him, but it was a rare occasion when he met someone who was. They tended to die off from fighting or just flat out avoided being near other people. He knew there were other villages like his parents' that housed older Fae, but the homes were warded against others finding them. Berkley assumed that if the Fae did that, then other species probably did too, or at least hid in very remote areas. The world had changed so much, so quickly, that some had chosen to isolate rather than try to adjust to the new world of cars, computers, and cell phones with cameras.

"Two thousand-ish, give or take a little bit. I don't remember when my birthday actually is. I remember being told it was in the winter. My parents did not celebrate my birth."

"Well, at least I'm not the oldest one anymore," Berkley replied, trying to lighten the sadness he saw on Doc's face. Doc was about seventeen hundred years older than him. It would be neat to hear the stories he could tell them. Hopefully now that Doc knew they would accept him, he would be more open to talking about his past. Berkley had the feeling that he had been alone and without anyone to really talk to for a long time, probably since he had been made to leave his tribe. It was hard forming strong friendships when you couldn't tell them a big part of your life.

Emma joined in. "Albert picked January sixteenth for his birthday. I told him he needed to have a day so we could celebrate."

"It doesn't have to be that day. I just picked a winter month and day; I didn't want it to interfere with Christmas," Doc protested.

"I think that sounds like a grand idea," Ian said cheerfully. "What do ye want to do for your birthday?"

"Oh, nothing big. Plus, aren't you guys going to be going to Scotland for a visit? I haven't ever had a birthday celebration; we don't need to change anything around for it this year!" Doc protested.

Berkley glanced at Ian, quickly communicating over their bond. "We've moved it back until February. Flights are cheaper then and it was a better time to visit his parents. Would you like to go out to eat or have something here? Ian and I can make that brisket you liked at Thanksgiving, or whatever else you might want," he offered. He had a feeling Doc would want to stay in; no one in town knew when his birthday was, so he probably didn't want a big deal made of it.

"I'd like it to be just the family at the house. Otherwise, we'll have everyone from town all over us. The brisket sounds delicious, thank you," Doc replied with a smile.

3

I an sat at the corner desk they had in their room. He was looking for flights to Scotland, trying to nail down a date. The flights were a little cheaper in February, probably because the weather was still iffy then. You could have a pop-up snow or hailstorm, or you could have sunny and close to fifty degrees Fahrenheit, or possibly even both in the space of a couple of days. His parents didn't have anything going on and told them they were available any time they wanted to come over. However, going during non-peak season also meant that they might not be able to get a straight flight over. He knew they would need to make it to New York and then fly over to Scotland, but he was hoping to avoid more than one stop or layover. He hated being stuck sitting in the airport. Scrolling through the flight options, he struggled to find one with a decent price, where he and Berkley could sit together, and with only one or two stops. It was frustrating. The times were a little ridiculous as well, especially considering they would want to arrive when the rental car place would be open. He also didn't fancy driving in the dark. It had been a while since he had visited and would prefer to have any driving done during the daytime as there were not a lot of streetlights once you got out of the city.

Giving up, Ian scooted the chair back and gave it a spin with his foot. He quickly pulled his feet up to sit crossed-legged on the seat. He was sure he looked ridiculous, but he was having fun as the room spun around him. After a few more spins, he was slightly dizzy and bored. Berkley was still sleeping. Ian picked up the toy airplane that he got in the Christmas White Elephant game. He had been a little disappointed when Shaye had stolen his hammock in the game, but the plane was fun to play with and Shaye let him use the hammock whenever he wanted. Ian glanced over at his sleeping mate, a mischievous smirk on his face. He wound the toy up, eyeing the path he wanted it to take. Letting go, he held his breath as the little toy flew toward their bed. He wasn't sure it was going to make it as it started to lose power. He watched as it started to dip and wobble when it reached the foot of their bed.

Yes! he shouted in his head. He had managed to land it right on Berkley's face. As it perched precariously on the tip of his nose, Berkley woke up. Ian started laughing as his mate's eyes crossed to look at the plane sitting on his nose. 'Really?' he asked Ian, grumpy amusement in his voice. Instead of knocking the toy off right away, Berkley's eyes squinted even harder looking at the toy. Gasping, he sat up, grabbing the plane as it fell.

"Ian, look at this!" Berkley said excitedly.

"What? Did I break it?" Ian asked, crossing the room to look at the toy. He didn't think he had overwound it.

"Nope. Look," Berkley told him, holding out the toy.

Ian took it, looking it over. "What am I looking for?" he asked, not seeing any cracks or damage.

"Look closer," Berkley instructed.

There were tiny scratches on the bottom...wait, no those

were words! "Good for two first-class plane tickets," he read, squinting. "What!" he exclaimed.

He rushed to their door and yanked it open. Poking his head out their bedroom door, he shouted down the hallway. "Shaye, get your butt over here!"

Her door opened and Shaye looked at him with an eyebrow raised. He held up the plane, shaking it a little. She started laughing as she turned to face back inside her room. "Rolf, they finally found it," she said. "Give him a minute to put on pants, and we'll be down," she told Ian, laughing as he made a face at her.

'Ye better put pants on as well,' Ian told Berkley grudgingly.

Shaye came out into the hallway a minute later, dragging her mate down to their room.

"It took you long enough," she teased as she walked through their door.

"Is this for real?" Ian asked.

Rolf nodded. "We knew you wanted to go see your parents, so we were hoping you would get it in the game. When Shaye ended up being the last one to pick and it was the last present, it was perfect," he replied with a big grin.

"It was Rolf's idea," Shaye added.

"What if we didn't win it?" Berkley questioned, amused.

"We still would have gotten you tickets and then someone else would have gotten a trip too," Rolf replied with a shrug.

"First class is too much," Ian protested. He had never flown first class. His business did well, but not so well that he threw money around on expensive plane tickets.

Rolf simply shook his head. "I have it all set up, you just have to call my travel person and give the dates you want to go," Rolf responded, handing Berkley a card with the contact information. They were getting the first-class tickets; he already warned his travel agent that they might try to get downgraded to cheaper seats and she had been instructed to keep them in first class.

"She does a great job with finding flights that work with the times you want, limited layovers, that kind of thing. It should make it a lot easier. Plus, if you do have extra time at the airport, you will be able to use the lounge. It makes sitting around an airport a little nicer. Ian, if you fly out of JFK and happen to have time waiting in the lounge and you get a little hungry, go up to the bar in the lounge and ask for a Bloody Marguerite."

"You mean a Bloody Mary?" Ian asked.

"Nope, Bloody Marguerite. If it's a paranormal or a human in the know who's working, they will give you blood. It's in a special glass, so the color will resemble a Bloody Mary. If it's a regular human, they'll be confused and ask if you wanted a Bloody Mary."

"Huh. I had no idea that even existed," Ian said.

"It's only in the lounges. They tried with the restaurants, but it didn't work out well and they stopped doing it," Rolf replied with a shrug.

"Well, thank ye for this," Ian said, a little overwhelmed by Rolf's generosity. He knew the man had lots of money, his house and land showed that, but he was giving them such a great gift. If they hadn't gotten the prize in the game, he still would have given them tickets.

'You helped Shaye whenever she needed you,' Rolf told Ian quietly, using the Clan link to speak to him telepathically. *'There is nothing that can thank you enough for that. This is just a way for me to say thank you for looking after my mate all those years. She would have been lost without you. Plus, Berkley is one of my oldest friends as well. We're family.'*

Ian blinked quickly, not wanting Shaye to think he was upset. He was glad she had found such a wonderful partner and he was so happy to be part of their lives.

Berkley was attempting to say goodbye to Ian before he went to work, but he was sorely tempted to drag him back to bed. They had gotten up early to help make breakfast for Doc's birthday. Ian was working from home today so that he could keep an eye on the brisket for dinner. After breakfast, Berkley had helped carry everything outside. He wanted to help get it set up before he left for work.

"I'll see you tonight," Berkley said, giving Ian one last kiss before walking back into the house. He turned around when he felt a pinch on his arse. Ian stood there grinning, mischief dancing in his eyes. "Hold that thought until tonight," Berkley told him sternly. "I'm going to be late opening the shop if I don't get going soon. I put a couple alarms on your phone to remind you to eat. There are some protein bars in the fridge that should be quick enough to grab."

"Thank ye, *mo ghaol*. Have a good day," Ian replied, kissing his man one more time. He thought today would be a good day; he was helping with dinner, but he also wanted to help keep an eye on the new puppy the house acquired.

It had been quite the surprise when Emma and Doc brought home a wolf-dog pup last night. The poor mother had been found shot in the National Park, where there was definitely a hunting ban. In fact, most of the area around here had no-hunting ordinances. A lot of the local woods belonged to Rolf, who had fences and No Hunting signs up as well. Some of the other wooded areas nearby, as well as the local and state parks, also did not allow hunting. A lot of this was due to the fact that there were several paranormals in the local governments who had helped declare the area hunting free. There were a lot of shifters in the area and a stray bullet could just as easily kill a real bear or a shifter. Gage, the town Sheriff and local paranormal Warden, was looking into the matter and making sure that No Hunting information was posted in all public buildings. Ian could tell they were worried it wasn't normal wildlife hunters or poachers, but hunters of the paranormal. He really hoped not. This area had never had a problem with hunters before, at least according to Rolf. It was one of the reasons he had liked the area so much. It felt safe.

He spritzed the meat with the apple juice one more time before closing the lid and moving over to work on the patio. The sun was shining bright without any clouds in the sky and the magic dome Berkley had placed over the area made it feel warmer. It wasn't a bad temperature to work outside. He opened his traveling case of tools; it had his mallet as well as his swivel knives, stamps, and bevelers organized by type and size, standing up in a display for easy use. He was going to try out a few new designs today on the scrap leather before he decided to attempt them on the nicer pieces he had. As he sorted through the scraps of leather, he grabbed a long piece that was a nice mix of flexible but strong. Ian had an idea of making a collar for the pup. He envisioned the leather with a silver buckle, maybe a moon with a wood and stream design tooled into the leather. The pup would need a collar and a tag sooner or later if they were going to bring him into town for socialization like Sam had recommended. It would also cause people to think he was simply a big dog, not as much of a threat, if the collar were on.

He cut the leather into a straight strip before measuring it out to the right length. He wanted to make the collar as comfortable as possible, so he grabbed an edge beveler to create a rounded edge all around the collar. He oiled the area where leather would bend over to secure the buckle to make sure the leather wouldn't crack. Using a small round punch, he created the holes where the rivets would be placed to secure the leather together. Grabbing his bag punch, he created the long hole where the prong of the buckle would slide through. Ian tested the bend in the leather and decided he needed to thin it a bit more for the rivets to fit. Using the skive tool, he tested it again and was happy with how it would secure. Moving to the other end of the strip, he punched holes for size adjustment. He debated using a scrap piece of leather to create the keeper but decided to use a metal one and add a D-ring for either tags or a leash when they were in town. He chose ones with the lowest profile, not wanting it to catch on anything when the pup eventually explored the outdoors. Now that the basic shape was done, he could get to his favorite part, the creative design. He was going to wing this one, he thought, not wanting to create a design and then trace it onto the leather. Grabbing a roll of clear packing tape, he turned the leather over to expose the back and applied a strip of tape to give it support during cutting so that the leather wouldn't spread and lose its shape. Flipping it back over, he grabbed his sponge and moistened the top of the leather, getting it ready to tool.

The back door opened and an exhausted-looking Emma walked out. "Morning, Ian. I was wondering if you could watch this guy for an hour or so while I get a nap? We didn't get much sleep last night."

"Of course," Ian agreed. "He can sleep in his blankets out here and I can get him a bottle if he's due. I'm actually working on a collar for him when he gets a wee bit bigger. I figured he would need one once we start taking him into town."

"Oh, Ian. That is so sweet of you! I'm sure it will be amazing." Emma smiled. "I just fed him, so he should stay in a food coma for a little bit. There is an extra bottle already made up in the fridge if he does get hungry. Thank you so much! I just need a little bit more sleep."

"Take as long as ye need," Ian told her. "We'll be fine."

He took the pup from her, arranging a pile of blankets to form a nest with a puppy pad on top and laid the pup down, making sure he was covered. It was a decent temperature out for him, but the pup was still small and would get cold easier. Ian took a moment to spray the brisket with the apple juice again before he went back to work on the collar, creating a woodland scene with a stream flowing through. He stamped a full moon overhead and was debating if he should create a few wolf shapes hidden among the trees. He had a little space left where he thought he could fit some. His hearing picked up on light whimpers though and he put his tools down to check on the pup. It looked like he had wet the pad and might be hungry again. Picking up the little guy first, Ian grabbed the soiled pad and threw it in the garbage cans on his way inside.

"Just a minute, little one. I'm going to heat up your bottle. No one likes to drink cold milk when it's chilly outside," Ian said. As the formula warmed, he grabbed a couple of the granola bars to eat. Cradling the pup in his arm, bottle and a new puppy pad in the other hand, Ian nudged the back door open and went to sit down to feed him. He was such a wee thing, Ian thought, watching him suckle. He fit quite easily in his hand. As the pup finished his bottle, his body relaxed into sleep again. Ian gave him a light kiss on his head before tucking him back into his little nest of a bed and tucking one of the blankets around his small body.

Ian had just finished attaching the buckle and hammering the rivets closed when he heard the back door open again.

"Ian, you are the best. I feel much better, but you should have woken me up! I didn't mean to sleep so long," Emma said, coming over to his impromptu work desk.

"Ye needed it. The pup ate again and has been sleeping," Ian told her.

"Is this the collar you were working on for him?" Emma asked, leaning over the table.

"Yup, it's for when he's a little bigger. I debated with putting the D-ring on but went with a small one in case we need to use a leash when we take him places. I can leave it plain or paint some of it, if ye wanted."

"It's beautiful, Ian," Emma exclaimed, looking at all the

details. "This is amazing. Thank you," she said, giving him a kiss on the cheek. "I'll take him inside and get going on the side dishes. Do you need anything?"

"I'm good, thank ye," Ian replied.

He cleaned up and put his tools away, keeping an eye on the brisket. Everyone seemed to arrive home about the same time, and he saw them helping set the table and get drinks ready. He checked the brisket for tenderness one last time, before grabbing the platter and removing it from the heat. Pushing the back door open, he took the meat in and thinly sliced it before shouting, "Dinner's ready!"

Berkley came in, giving him a kiss, getting their plates ready. It was nice to have everyone together on a day other than Sunday, he thought. Dinner was followed by games, gifts, and dessert. Ian yawned, ready to snuggle with Berkley in their bed.

"Ye ready to head upstairs?" Ian asked, leaning his head against Berkley's shoulder.

"Yes. Should we offer to take the pup so they can have alone time?" he asked in a whisper.

"Emma already asked Tess," Ian said, standing to hold out a hand to pull Berkley up. "Let's go snuggle."

They trudged up the stairs, tired from the long day, but happy with how it had gone. Standing at the sink, brushing their teeth, Ian wondered if he should bring up the question that had been bugging him about Berkley's family. He spit out the toothpaste and then swished with water before talking.

"Ber, can I ask you a question?"

"Always," Berkley answered, the words a little muffled by the toothbrush and goo in his mouth.

"Do… Are you…" Ian paused not quite sure how to ask what had been bothering him.

"Wah?" Berkley asked, toothbrush still in his mouth.

Ian waited until his lover was done brushing his back

teeth. He didn't need to cause him to accidentally stab himself with the toothbrush. "Are ye not talking to your family? Or do they no' like vampires?" He couldn't figure out Berkley's family dynamics. He was also wondering why he hadn't met them yet. Oh, he knew they were in England, but they could talk on the phone or do a video call, something. Berkley had already met his aunt and uncle on video call and talked to his parents over the phone. Heck, Clara had called in between rehearsals and said hi. They were mates, he would have thought that just like when humans were serious about someone, he would have been introduced to his family. Most paranormals celebrated babies and finding mates. Unless Berkley didn't want Ian to meet his family, he thought glumly.

Berkley spit out the toothpaste, wiping his mouth. "I don't think they have anything against vampires, not sure if they've met one or not. Why? Where is this coming from?" Berkley was honestly confused. He wasn't sure why Ian would think his parents didn't like vampires. He certainly hadn't ever said anything like that.

"You don't talk about them much. I've never met them, not even just a phone conversation," Ian told him.

Berkley looked at Ian, noticing that he was genuinely upset by this, hurt in his eyes. He had somehow, inadvertently, hurt Ian's feelings. He wasn't sure what the correct response was here. He had never had a relationship before Ian and his family wasn't known for talking out their emotions.

"We're not big talkers," Berkley told him. "I left them a voicemail letting them know I had mated, but I haven't really talked to them since then. We're pretty bad at staying in touch."

Ian huffed out a sigh. "Okay," he replied, a little defeated. He was hoping to get some insight into why he hadn't talked or met with any of them yet. At least one should be curious about Berkley's life, he reasoned. He was tired and didn't want to escalate this, so he was going to go to sleep and see how he felt in the morning. "Night," he said quietly, giving Berkley a quick kiss before crawling under the covers.

Berkley watched his partner's body, curled up and faced away from him. He grabbed the floss, finishing his nightly routine. He had thought he had explained it okay, but clearly, he had made things worse.

'Shaye? Can I ask you a question?' he asked, reaching out over the Clan link. She had known Ian the longest and might be able to tell him what he did wrong.

'Sure. Is everything okay?'

'Maybe? I think I messed up with Ian, but I'm not sure how or what to do to fix it,' Berkley admitted.

'Tell me what happened,' Shaye responded.

'He asked if I wasn't talking to my family; like fighting, I think. Or if they didn't like vampires. I told him no; we just don't talk a lot.'

'Hm,' Shaye said, pausing for a minute before continuing. 'Has Ian met any of your family yet?'

'No. I called and left a voicemail at my parents' house, but that was it. I haven't heard back from them yet. We really aren't big talkers,' he stressed.

'Have you met Ian's family?'

'Yeah. I had a video call with his aunt and uncle and a quick phone call with his parents. Just to introduce me and to say we were coming for a visit sometime soon. His cousin called to say hi too,' Berkley said.

'Berkley,' she sighed. 'My guess is he is wondering if you are ashamed of him, or of him being a vampire, or if they're speciesist. I know you aren't, I can feel that, and he should be able to as well, but he must be feeling insecure about this. I'd sit down and talk to him, explain the why,' Shaye advised.

'It's not really a big deal,' he protested. 'The Fae aren't big into showing a lot of affection, more of a standoffish kind of lot. We don't talk a lot. There were days no one spoke other than to ask where *something was in my house. We didn't discuss our feelings, didn't ask how our day was. It was more like coexisting with subdued feelings of fondness. I don't even know if I have the updated phone numbers for my siblings or any cousins, for that matter. I just leave a message at my parents', and they pass it on whenever someone calls in. It's a pretty common practice, at least in our village. The only time there's a big effort to get in contact with someone would be if there's a baby born.'*

'Okay, so while that may be normal to you, it's not for Ian. I would talk to him and try to explain it a little better so that he doesn't think it has to do with him,' Shaye replied.

'I'm sure when my parents heard the message, they were happy for me and passed the information on. If they had nothing new to report, then they wouldn't normally call me back,' Berkley explained.

'I get that, I do. But Ian clearly doesn't. After you talk to him, an easy way to fix this might be getting updated numbers from your parents and starting a group text for your family. That way you could keep in contact easier and faster, but without a lot of phone calls or in-person meetings, if that's easier for them,' she said. 'Plus, Ian could say hello as well if you added him to the group.'

'Alright. That's not a bad idea. I'll email or text my mom to ask for the information; I'll probably get a faster response that way. I'll go try to explain it better to Ian. Thanks,' Berkley added, still a little confused on why it was such a big deal that Ian hadn't spoken with his family yet. Relationships outside of the Fae definitely required more work. He could remember a few arguments with Sam or Rolf over the years over something similar, now that he thought about it.

Berkley threw the floss out, rinsing with mouthwash before walking over to the bed. He could tell Ian was still awake, no matter how still he was being, his body wasn't relaxed at all. Climbing in, he snuggled up to Ian, being the big spoon.

"My family isn't speciesist as far as I know," he started. "I don't believe they have met many other species since they don't really leave the village. I have a few cousins who have left, and my siblings have gone on adventures before, but they never brought up meeting different paranormals.

"I think they are probably happy that I found my mate, and it won't matter to them that you're a vampire. The Fae are...not a very open group of people when it comes to showing affection or even talking to each other. As a whole, physical affection isn't shown much outside of sex, so no hand-holding, no random kisses, no hugs, even among the children. We're kind of an awkward people. We love each other. But we certainly don't show it well, not like most other people seem to do. I was surprised by a pat on the back and a quick hug when I left home. That carries over to our interactions as well. I'm sure Mom passed on the message and was happy about it, but if she didn't have any news to add, she wouldn't have felt the need to call back. I gave out Rolf's address for mail when I decided to stay in Rockfort with Sam and Rolf. I sent a letter home saying that's where any mail could be sent. I think I got a letter maybe once every few years. When Maddie, my sister, had a child, I got a letter. When Isaac, my brother, left the village, I got a letter. When they finally got a landline and then internet many, many years later, I got a letter. It's not that they don't care, it's that they don't know how to show it like you all do. I promise it has nothing to do with you," Berkley swore, leaning in to nuzzle his nose against Ian's neck.

"Shaye recommended getting everyone's cell phone numbers from Mom and setting up a group chat, so that this isn't a problem again. You can jump in there and I can introduce you, or I can set up a time to video call with them to introduce you to at least my mom and dad. Okay? You'll see it has nothing to do with you. You're my fated, they'll love you in their own quiet way because I love you."

Ian rolled over, tucking his head into Berkley's shoulder

and wrapping an arm around his waist. "Okay," he whis-pered. "Sorry for being so needy," he apologized.

"You're not being needy. I'm sorry for not realizing that it would bother you. It's just how the Fae are, and I'm used to it when dealing with my family. Just ask Rolf and Sam. We butted heads over my lack of emotional and verbal connec-tion in the beginning. I've gotten loads better, but I still slip when dealing with my birth family," Berkley said.

"I love you just how you are. I should have said some-thing sooner," Ian admitted. "I knew you didn't grow up the same. I forgot just how different it was and may have overre-acted," he admitted, giving Berkley a kiss to his chest.

4

Sunday nights were his favorite, Ian thought as he watched everyone interact around the dinner table. It got a little loud sometimes, but it was a happy loud. It was the one night during the week when they were all home and were able to get together and share dinner; the clinic and library were closed, Sam had someone cover his duties at the brewery after the lunch rush, and Berkley closed the shop early. Gawain was the only one who was bad at attending the Sunday dinners, but now that Merri was here, she would drag him from his research and make him join them. Ian had instituted game night on Sundays after everyone agreed to having family dinner on that day. It gave them all time to relax and hang out with each other. His hope was that it would have everyone end the week on a good note and be able to start the new week relaxed. They all loved their jobs, but a case of the Mondays hit them all at some point.

Since they were all together, it gave them time to catch up and share any news. Tonight, Ian and Berkley had something to share, but they were going to wait until after dessert. They had finally booked tickets to fly to Scotland to see Ian's parents.

Berkley squeezed Ian's hand, letting him know it was a good time to say something. Ian smiled at him before turning back to the table.

"We finally set a date to see my parents. We'll be leaving in a couple of weeks," Ian said.

"I'm going to close the store while we're gone and put a notice that orders are on hold for the moment on the online shop," Berkley added. "I don't want you guys having to cover while I'm out. It's normally the slow part of the season, so it would just be a lot of sitting around. If someone still submits an order, it can wait until we get back."

"You'll have to send us pictures," Shaye said. "I want to go see Scotland, especially Loch Ness, one day. And make sure you let us know when you land!" With the attacks on Rolf and Tess and Sam, she was both happy Ian would be able to see his family, but worried that they would be so far away. She could sense everyone in the Clan's well-being. She knew it worked up to a couple hundred miles but had no idea if her reach would extend across the ocean. It made her a little nervous that if they were hurt, they would be too far away for her to help.

"I will send you so many pictures!" Ian promised. He couldn't wait until they could plan a big family trip and see his home country. He thought maybe they could make it a two-week trip with the whole family and fit in England too. He was sure Berkley and Emma had plenty of places to show them.

Doc looked at Emma, who nodded in return. "I know you guys are leaving soon, but before you go, there is something we wanted to talk to you about," Doc said, placing his fork down and grabbing Emma's hand. "Tonight's as good as any, since you are all here."

Emma stood, pulling Doc up with her. "Let's all go to the living room and sit down. I need to grab a bottle for the puppy and then I'll join you."

Ian followed Berkley into the living room. Berkley sat in one of the recliners and Ian plopped on the floor in front of him. *'There is another chair right next to me,'* Berkley pointed out dryly, looking down at his mate who was currently sitting on top of his feet.

'I know. I want to be close to you though. Now spread your legs for me.' He leered up at Berkley, lifting his arse just enough for Berkley to pull his feet out from under him.

Berkley shook his head, a small smile on his face, but he spread his legs wider, allowing Ian to scoot back so that he was encased between Berkley's legs. He had no idea why Ian loved sitting like this, but whenever they were just relaxing, most times he ended up snuggling in this position. Leaning down, he pressed a kiss to the top of Ian's head before sitting back. He let his fingers lazily run through the red hair, loving how soft it felt against his fingers.

Emma came into the room, holding a tiny bottle. She bent to pick up the puppy out of his little mound of blankets before sitting next to Doc.

'Do you think she's pregnant?' Ian asked. He wasn't certain what they could want to talk to everyone about. They all lived together so it wasn't like they wouldn't have heard if they had any other big news. If they were expecting, they were going to be busy with a wolf-dog pup and a baby at the same time. Not that they wouldn't all help out. He would be more than happy to puppy or babysit.

Berkley looked at them closely, opening his magic to study their auras. *'It doesn't look like it,'* he replied. *'If she was pregnant, I should be able to see another aura.'*

"So...uh...right...I wanted to ask...you can say no, you don't have to say yes...it was just an idea," Doc began, for once not very coherent.

Shaye looked over at Ian, an eyebrow raised. Ian shook his head at her silent question. He had no idea what was going on. She shrugged her shoulders in response, not knowing either.

Emma sighed. "What Albert is trying to get at is that he is an alicorn—"

"We know that already, Mom," Rolf interjected.

"And what that comes with is what we wanted to talk to you about. If you can keep from interrupting, son," Emma gently scolded Rolf.

"Sorry," Rolf replied sheepishly.

"There are a few of us rare shifters that belong to a bit of a secret forum. It's buried in the dark web, under magical and technological safeguards. Everything is kept rather vague, no mention of locations, names, or species just in case hunters would find it. Even with us not trying to be specific, there are things on there that would be a gold mine for them, and we really don't want that. Anyway, after we formed the Clan bond, my beast became harder to control. He's always been a bit of a separate entity, not like a normal shifter. I couldn't figure out what was causing him to act out. The day I closed the office it was because he had taken control and wouldn't let me change back."

"Where were you?" Tess asked. She didn't think he would have fit in his house well, but there was no way he could have gone outside without being noticed especially since he hadn't had the concealment spell on his pendant yet.

"In my garage. It's why I never park in there, it's set up for when I need to let my beast out," Doc replied.

"I always thought you just had a bunch of junk stored in there," Sam confessed.

Doc shook his head. "Since I was stuck, I used the tablet and stylus that I keep in there to do some research. I found the start of a thread that stated similar problems. Emma came over, found me, and settled my beast enough that I could change back. She helped look through the forum for more information. He wouldn't shut up about 'mine' for days after

Sam was brought home. It took me a bit to figure out what the problem was; it turns out that my beast was upset because it thought that a claiming bond had been started with the telepathic link we shared to save Sam. He wanted to claim you all as his tribe, even though we had the Clan bond already. He's a bit greedy, I guess. Emma helped calm him down again by using the link to show him you were all safe and healthy. It hadn't even crossed my mind to do that," he admitted.

Sam looked worried. He didn't want saving him to have caused any problems for a member of his family.

"No, Sam," Doc said in response to Sam's face. "It's no one's fault. I had no idea such a thing was even possible. It might be a good thing though, but this is where my question comes into play."

He stopped again, looking worried now. Emma was still holding the pup, so she leaned her head against her mate's shoulder in comfort. Ian couldn't begin to fathom what had Doc so worked up.

"It'll be fine. Just tell them," Emma told Doc, kissing the end of his nose.

"So, some of the rarer paranormals have extra…features," he began. "Not really physical features, but gifts, I guess you could call them. It's been hard finding information because there aren't a lot of us, it seems like we're one-offs most of the time. What I have been able to find so far, is information that would be catastrophic in the wrong hands, so that may be why there isn't a lot more readily available. Whatever the reason, it took me a while to figure out that I was immortal. When Emma agreed to be my mate, she also became immortal, similar to when the Fae mate."

Ian looked around the group. Rolf looked sad; it was hard knowing that you would die before your parent. Plus, half of the Clan would be gone, a fact that Ian had been steadfastly ignoring since mating with Berkley. He could never, ever regret mating with his Fae, but the thought of their friends and family passing on and leaving them alone was depressing. At least they would have Emma and Doc now, he thought. Emma must have been devastated when she learned about it though, and he wondered if that had been one of the reasons their mating had taken a couple of months to complete. "There was some information that made it seem like it wasn't just my mate that I could share it with. I did some more digging, but it wasn't until my birthday that I knew enough to bring it up with you. The forum came through and sent me some old documents that illustrated a claiming ceremony. It seems shockingly easy. It starts with creating a telepathic link to someone in both my forms. The other person must be completely aware of who and what the paranormal is and consent, or a true bond won't form. Once I initiate it, the other person or people, must then reach out telepathically from their side and that forms the tribe link/bond. The link needs to be used in both my animal and human form for it to take. It would be like the Clan bond, so a little redundant, I know, but the beast really wants it."

"If it will calm him down, I don't think any of us would have a problem with it," Rolf said.

"Thank you," Doc said hesitantly, pausing for a moment before continuing. "It's not just the link though. That is just the first part of the ceremony. The rest would be in order to share my immortality with you. And keep in mind that this information was given to me by an anonymous source from very old documents, so I can't guarantee it would work. While it would be great to keep you safe because you guys seem to get hurt pretty frequently, it would also draw the wrong type of attention to you if it ever became known that you were immortal and not mated to an immortal species. Not to mention the potential added threat of hunters."

"What's the second part of the ceremony?" Tess asked, curious. Doc seemed quite worried about this secondary part, so she guessed it wasn't as simple as a telepathic link.

"It's a little similar to the Clan bond, but in reverse. You would be the ones drinking. I would need to put some of my blood in a vessel. It isn't very clear on the container, just that it needs to be 'held in fond regard.' I need to meditate over it while focusing on my intent to share my immortality and say a spell. I would love if Berkley and Tess could read it over and make sure that there isn't anything harmful hiding in it. I have some minor healing magic, but it's innate, I don't really use spells."

"I can look it over," Berkley agreed, seeing Tess nod as well. He was interested to see how the spell was worded. Not all paranormals had useable magic; they were all a little magical given their paranormal status and some had extra gifts like healing, speed, and telepathy, but those weren't the same as having and shaping magic. For example, Ian was magical to him, but to everyone else he was a vampire who had an extra gift of speed. The magic was present in his species status and in the gift of his speed, but it was passive in that he couldn't actively use magic to create a spell.

"Thank you," Doc said, relieved. "I have a copy of it, I'll be right back," he said as he stood to run up to his room.

Emma looked at them all. "We don't want you to feel any pressure. We would of course love it if we could all be together forever. However, ultimately it is up to you to decide what is best for you and your mate. We've adopted all of you, and as your parents we just want you to be happy," Emma added with a smile.

"What do you think of Doc's proposal?" Ian asked Berkley as they lay in bed. He had rolled on his side so he could talk to him. After Doc explained everything, he said he would let them think about it and to let him know later what their decisions were. He didn't want to pressure them at all, so he said he would be up in his room for the rest of the night if anyone had questions.

"I've never heard of such a thing, but then again, I haven't really met any of the extremely rare paranormals either. Even if I had met one in passing, I wouldn't be good enough friends with them for them to trust me with that information. I can generally sense if someone's a paranormal and some- times what their species is. With Doc, I could tell he was para- normal, but never what kind, so I would assume it would be the same with the other rare ones. It's probably a safety feature they don't even know they have," Berkley responded.

"I mean, I'm already mated to you, so I have immortality, right? I wouldn't need to do the ceremony to achieve it. We have the Clan bond already too." Ever since they had mated, Ian hadn't wanted to drink from anyone else. He knew there were blood bags in the house for emergencies, but he'd rather go hungry for a little bit than taste someone else. Even with the blood being in a cup or something, he didn't want any other source than Berkley.

"Love, it would be alright if you drank. I know it has nothing to do with our bond. There will be times you will probably need to drink from a blood bag or someone else," Berkley told him. He didn't want Ian to get stuck needing it and not be willing to take what he needed.

"It just feels wrong," Ian muttered. He was mated, and in his mind that commitment encompassed all aspects of his life, not just sex.

"What do you think about Shaye and Rolf?" Berkley asked.

"What do ye mean?"

"Well, I don't think they would get enough nutrition if they only drank from each other, so they need to use other blood. Do you think any less of them or think they are cheating on each other?" Berkley questioned, trying to get Ian to see his point.

"No, I don't think that. That's what they need to survive, and they dinnae have sex with anyone else since they're mated so there's no cheating. It's different," he said grumpily.

"It's not, love. Just because you have a mate you can drink from without having to go to another source, doesn't mean it's any different. I love that you're so committed to me, I really do. But I don't want it to ever affect your health or your happiness.

"I think the Clan bond only includes Doc right now, not his animal side. It is odd that they are so separate. I haven't heard of that before. I wonder if my family has anything in the village archives that might help," Berkley pondered. "They used to collect old documents, not sure if they still do. I don't mind committing to another family link, especially if it would help Doc out. Plus, maybe you'll get double coverage on the immortality thing," he joked.

"I don't think that's how that works," Ian replied with an eye roll.

"No, probably not. I would love it though if our friends could live as long as us. I think this will probably be a case of everyone does it together, or it won't happen."

"Nope. I'm making Shaye and Tess do it. If I can hae my best friends forever, I'm going to convince them to do it," Ian said resolutely. He didn't know how he would be able to watch his little sister and friend pass away. He had been ignoring the fact that they had an expiration date and he didn't. Doc's confession tonight had made him face it and he was a little grumpy about that.

"You can't make them," Berkley protested with a laugh. "Although I'm sure Rolf will want to so he won't have to leave his mom. Shaye finally has the family she always dreamed of, so I'm sure she will vote to do it. I can see Tess and Sam committing as well, especially if Rolf and Shaye do. And not to bring it up again, but if you are willing, they may be as well. Gawain and Merri...I'm not sure. Gawain gets so caught up in his research that he probably wouldn't even notice any difference to his life other than he could keep doing what he loves forever. Merri though…this is her first time away from her birth family and I could see that playing a factor in her choice. She would have Tess but eventually lose the rest of her family to old age. I don't know her well enough yet to know if having Tess and us would be enough to convince her. She hasn't been here very long to form the same tight bonds that the rest of us have. It will come in time, but I don't know if the promise of that will be enough," Berkley added.

"Humph," Ian grunted. "We dinnae even hae game night," he grouched.

Berkley took a good look at his pouty mate. "Come here, love," he said, pulling Ian closer, loving the hitch in his breath as he grabbed him by his cheeks. "What has you so grumpy? You're normally my sunshine."

Ian snuggled in, tucking his head under Berkley's chin before answering. "I love ye, never doubt that. But I've been ignoring that the rest of them wouldn't live as long as us. Shaye and Tess hae been my family. Shaye is like my little sister. It didn't bother me as much when we all had an end date, as it were, but when we mated and I got immortality, it hit me hard. Now Doc has a solution and the thought that they might say no is killing me," Ian admitted. He wasn't sure how to explain it. Shaye and Tess were his ride-or-dies, much like he thought Sam and Rolf were Berkley's.

Berkley kissed the top of Ian's head. "Why don't you talk to them tomorrow? It might make you feel better."

"Yeah," Ian replied, still a little sullen.

"We can have our own game night," Berkley said with a little smile. He knew just the thing to get Ian out of his funk.

"What did ye want to play?" Ian asked.

Berkley slid his hand slowly down Ian's chest, feeling the beat of his heart speed up, the pause in the rise of his chest as his breath caught. He smirked as Ian's head popped up, his pupils blown, as he lightly touched his mate's cock through his jeans.

"Ber—" Ian moaned, his hips thrusting in an attempt to get more friction.

"Yes, dear?" Berkley asked innocently.

"Inside my pants, please," Ian begged. He grabbed Berkley's hips, pulling him closer.

"Don't you want to play the game?"

"Wha—what game?" Ian gasped out as Berkley slid his hand into his pants, teasing the tip of his cock.

"Who can last longer," Berkley replied.

Ian grabbed Berkley's long hair, bunching the platinum strands in his fist, pulling his mouth down to his. Berkley pushed on Ian's shoulder until he rolled on his back, Berkley following to roll on top of him. He lightly dragged his teeth across Ian's bottom lip, ravaging his mouth, plunging and twisting his tongue against Ian's. Goodness, he loved kissing his mate. Berkley removed his hand from Ian's cock, Ian making a sound of protest, his hips chasing after his touch. Pushing up the hem of Ian's shirt to reveal the skin underneath as he went, Berkley licked his way up from the defined V of Ian's hips, across the six-pack abs, to the tight pink nubs of his nipples. He loved that Ian was pierced here, little bars that called out for his tongue and teeth to play. Berkley leaned on one elbow, lifting his hips away from Ian so he had room to slide his hand back into Ian's jeans, lightly circling his cock. Ian's hips rose up, seeking friction. Berkley gently grasped one end of the barbell with his teeth, giving it a little tug.

"That's cheating," Ian gasped. "Ye know they're super sensitive."

Berkley chuckled, his hand releasing Ian's cock to work his pants down his hips. Ian pushed his hand away, shoving his own pants and underwear down. Berkley watched as Ian's uncut dick popped back up, smacking himself in the stomach. It was thick and long, the tip peeking out already glistening with precum. Berkley gave Ian's nipples one last pinch before kissing his way back down to that glorious cock. He couldn't wait to taste it again, but he took his time, driving his mate crazy with little kisses and nips across his stomach. When he finally reached his destination, Berkley gently licked and kissed around Ian's shaft. Pulling the foreskin back, he ran his tongue around the head, collecting the liquid that had gathered there.

"You always taste so good, mate," Berkley said before opening his mouth wide to take him in.

Ian watched, gasping as Berkley's mouth closed around him. His mouth was so warm, his lips stretched tight around Ian's girth. Berkley was still teasing him though, his tongue gently moving against his length, only slightly moving his head. Ian needed more, more pressure, more thrusts, he needed it harder. Gripping Berkley's hair, he shoved his head down to get deeper into that warmth. When his partner gagged a little, Ian pulled back.

'*Sorry, mo ghaol,*' Ian said, moving a little more gently.

Berkley looked at him as he started to deep throat Ian's length. Those gorgeous purple-blue eyes watered a little, but then Ian was all the way in, his cock being massaged by Berkley's throat as he swallowed. He reached a hand down, pressing gently against Berkley's throat, eager to feel his cock through the skin. God that was hot. He let go, moving to ruck up Berkley's t-shirt, finding his tight nipples. Gently rolling them between his fingers, Ian was in pleasure overload. His mate had gotten so good at sucking him.

"Up," Ian demanded. "I want your clothes off."

Berkley took Ian's cock deep in his throat one last time, humming around the length, ramping up Ian's need.

"No, not yet," Ian snarled, pulling Berkley off by his hair. "My turn." He wrapped a leg around Berkley's waist and flipped them. He sat, straddling Berkley's hips before pulling his shirt off. Berkley reached out, trying to get Ian's nipples again, but Ian leaned farther back, his ass now rubbing along the hard cock pressing against him still trapped behind pants. Scooting backward, he undid Berkley's jeans button and carefully lowered the zipper. Pulling out Berkley's dick, Ian licked his lips at the sight. His mate's shaft was just a little shorter than his own, but Berkley was still large, and he had a girth that was even greater than Ian's. Bending down, he licked a path from the balls to the tip of his dick, Berkley moaning. Surging forward, Ian kissed his man, claiming his mouth. He lightly stroked, making sure to leave his hand loose, not quite tight enough to give Berkley the friction he craved. Berkley's hand moved in between them, grabbing Ian's dick, gripping it tight, stroking. Ian enjoyed the feel of the callused hand on him before pulling back and spitting in his hand. He spread the moisture over Berkley's head before spitting on his own cock. Leaning down he took Berkley's mouth in another kiss, their tongues tangling together, as Ian gripped both their cocks in his hand and jerked them off. Ian hissed as Berkley reached up, tugging on his barbells, sending shocks of pleasure down to his balls.

'*Soon,*' Berkley panted.

Ian added a twist to his strokes, just the way he knew Berkley liked it. He gave him one last kiss, moving his mouth over to lick his mate's neck. '*Yes,*' Berkley cried as Ian's teeth slid into his skin, drinking from him. Ian drew a couple of deep swallows before feeling the heat of Berkley's release. Not wanting to overstimulate him, Ian let go of Berkley's spent dick. Using the cum that had leaked onto his hand, Ian stroked himself faster, feeling his balls draw up before shooting over his mate. Licking the bite marks closed, Ian collapsed on top of Berkley, both of their chests heaving. Ian lay there breathing in their combined scent, endorphins chasing away any thoughts.

Berkley smiled drowsily at him, his muscles loose, his

body well pleasured and ready for sleep. Ian leaned down to give him a kiss before pulling back. Berkley reached out for him. "I'll be right back," Ian said, pressing a kiss to his forehead. Running into the bathroom, he turned on the hot water, getting a washcloth to wipe himself clean. Getting another one wet, he walked back into their bedroom and cleaned Berkley's skin, making sure he wouldn't wake with dried cum on him. Nothing was nastier than having that dried on your skin and stuck in your hairs. His guy barely stirred, already asleep. Ian tossed the washcloth back toward the bathroom before climbing into bed and pulling the covers over both of them.

"Night, love ye," he whispered, curling around Berkley.

5

Berkley was at work, but Ian wanted to stay home today. He wasn't going to be the best for smiling at customers this morning and he didn't want to take his bad mood out on Berkley either. He hadn't resolved anything in his own mind over Doc's offer. On one hand, he loved Doc. He was part of their family and Ian wanted him to feel fully accepted. Berkley seemed to have no problem with Ian drinking from someone else. Shite, Ian himself had no problem with Shaye and Rolf drinking the blood bags Doc got for them. It just was different when it came to him. In his mind, everything he was or had belonged to Berkley. Even his bites. He hadn't been exactly virginal when he came into their mating, having had quite a few years between turning and meeting Berkley. He was the more experienced between the two of them. He guessed that he was trying to show his mate that he was fully committed to him, that he didn't want anyone else, not even for substance? Ian didn't even know himself; he just knew that drinking anyone else's blood seemed wrong. It was ridiculous, he knew that. Mates didn't stray, that wasn't how fated mates worked. This block was all in Ian's own head.

He had tried to grab Shaye and Tess this morning to talk

to them about Doc's offer. He wanted to convince them to accept it. He didn't want to live forever and lose his best friends. He imagined Berkley felt the same, but on the other hand, Berkley had always known that any friends he made would probably die before him. Ian had only had a few months since their mating in November to come to terms with this knowledge. He'd always expected to die around the same time as any paranormal friends.

Both of his girls were running late, rushing out the door saying they would talk to him about it tonight. He knew they would need to discuss it with their own mates first, if they hadn't already, but he really wanted to get it settled. It would make it easier to drink someone else's blood if it meant that his friends would be around to share this life with him forever.

Ian tried working on some bracelet designs that he had in mind for the spring market. Berkley was selling his items in the Winged Potter, but Ian thought he might make some good sales at the farmer's market. The spring and winter markets were supposed to have a lot of craft items for sale. During the summer, Rolf had told him it was probably ninety percent produce and other farmer's market types of items, with only ten percent being craft goods. It was closer to eighty to ninety percent craft and gift items for sale in the spring and winter. After botching a couple of designs, Ian put away the leatherwork and went inside the house.

"Emma, do ye need any help wi' the wee pup today?" Ian asked, finding Emma in the kitchen.

"I don't think so," she replied. "I'm home today and he actually slept for several hours at a time last night, so I'm not too tired. Thank you for asking though."

Ian went up to his room and made the bed. Well, he just kind of threw the covers up over the bed. There wasn't a lot of tucking or smoothing of the blankets, but it was about as made as their bed ever was. He refilled the soap dispenser in their bathroom, as it was almost empty. Their laundry basket was overflowing, so he decided that he might as well do something useful today. Bending over, he grabbed the socks that always seemed to find their way under their bed. It was a mix of his and Berkley's, so at least he wasn't the only one making a mess in their room, he thought. Berkley liked everything neat and tidy, but for some reason socks didn't seem to count. Dragging the basket downstairs, he threw in a load. He added the detergent and set it to cold. Personally, he never sorted the lights and darks. Most of his clothes were colorful and there were only socks and a few undershirts that he owned in white, so he didn't see the point in doing different washes.

While the first load went through, Ian grabbed his laptop, thinking he would check his email and update some of the items for sale on his website. He needed to get more small knives up online, he thought to himself. He had his portable forge and could probably get a couple started today, especially if they were fixed blade types. He needed to grab some propane though, as he didn't have a full tank and he didn't want to steal the one off the grill. He didn't like traveling with a full tank ever since someone had hit his trailer a few years ago. Luckily only the trailer had been damaged and the propane tank hadn't been affected, but it had caused him to only travel with an empty tank. No reason to ask for a fire on top of a wreck.

"Emma? Do you know if there is somewhere that will refill propane tanks nearby?" Ian asked as he went back into the kitchen.

"There is! If you head west out of town, there's a place called Barry's. Maybe ten miles down the road? I just heard someone talking about it at the bookstore last weekend. Why?"

"I need a refill. I think I'm going to set up my forge in the backyard and try to get some work done."

"Aren't forges big?" Emma asked, curious. She didn't know much of forges outside of the ones that her father and Douglas, her farm's caretaker used. Both were large coal-burning forges, built into their own buildings away from the house.

"They can be. This one is a travel version and runs on propane. I can't make anything large with it, but I can make some knives and other smaller items. I was thinking of getting some knives made for the online shop and the spring market. Maybe some small candle holders as well. I may be able to swing those. I'll run down and get my tank refilled and then I'll be working in the backyard. If you need anything, just come and get me," Ian said, grabbing his keys from the key rack they had by the back door.

Ian would probably ditch his jacket once he got back to the house. He knew once he got going, he would be hot.

Placing the empty propane tank in the bed of his truck, Ian drove down to Barry's. It was a small roadside place, a little run-down. It did however have a large propane tank and was advertising refills. Getting out of the truck, Ian pulled the tank out of the bed and walked over to the refilling station. An older man wearing a pair of coveralls came out of the small building.

"Watcha need?" a gravely voice asked around a wad of chew in his cheek. The smell of his cologne was overpowering, filling Ian's nose until he couldn't smell anything else.

"I need to get a propane refill," Ian answered.

The man grunted and held out a hand for Ian's tank.

"Twenty dollars. You can pay inside," the man barked at him.

Not the friendliest guy, was he? Ian thought to himself. He watched to make sure the man actually hooked up his tank as he walked inside the small building. There was a small run-down soda machine, looking like it was on its last legs. The counter was beat up, knicks and chunks taken out of the old laminate. There was a young girl sitting behind the register.

"What were you getting today?" she asked.

"Propane tank refill," Ian replied.

"Did Grandpa say how much it was?"

"Twenty dollars," Ian answered, handing over cash. He didn't want to use his credit card here. "Thanks."

Ian walked back outside, seeing that the man was almost done with the tank. Turning off the machine, he handed it to Ian.

"You pay?" he asked.

Ian nodded, taking the tank from the grumpy gentleman as he thrust it at him. "Thanks," Ian said before bringing it over to his truck, setting it in the bed and using straps to hold it in place. He didn't need the tank rolling around. Driving home only took a few minutes, he seemed to hit all the green lights in the downtown area. He saw Berkely in the store and waved, but it looked like he was dealing with customers, so he kept driving.

Pulling into the driveway, Ian was excited. He hadn't worked with his forge in a while, and he was eager to see what he could make today. Walking into the backyard, he placed the tank to the left of the fireplace. He didn't want to get too close to the hammock pavilion or the house. Not that he ever let it get out of control, but he wanted to be safe. He figured the hearth could serve as a table for his tools and to keep the fire extinguisher close.

Grabbing the forge, he placed it on the hearth before going back for the stand. As he set it up, Ian went through his normal safety check of the forge since he hadn't used it for a couple of months. Everything looked solid, nothing cracked or broken. Checking the hoses and connections for wear, he was happy to see that they looked in good shape. After connecting the tank to the forge, he ran inside the house to change into his thicker pair of jeans and a long-sleeve cotton shirt, ditching his coat. The magical dome Berkley had cast over the patio area helped keep heat in during cooler days, so he was anticipating getting warm. He grabbed the outdoor fire extinguisher from the storage bin by the fireplace on his way back and placed it on the hearth.

Moving back to his trailer, Ian sighed as he looked at the mess. The forge had been placed near the entrance; however, the anvil, his tools, and safety equipment were scattered everywhere. It was normally more organized, but he had been in a rush to get here after his last gig. He had made it to Rolf's house just in time for the fight against Vlad, helping his friends win. Afterward, he had been distracted by a new mate, Thanksgiving, the attack on Sam, then the Christmas and New Year celebrations. He had been able to grab his leatherworking items but hadn't made the time to straighten the rest out.

This might take a while, Ian thought as he spotted the anvil all the way in the back. He would pull everything out and then try to sort it quickly so he could get some actual work done today, he reasoned as he started moving things out onto the grass. This should teach him not to leave cleaning up until the last minute. He worked on the right side of the trailer first, finally reaching the anvil. Ian grunted as he picked up the heavy, awkwardly shaped item. His anvil had been made with an attached base so he could use it at fairs and festivals without having to worry about finding a platform for it. It was a good thing he had paranormal strength or moving it would have been difficult. He made sure to place it on a flat surface on the patio so that it didn't rock or wiggle when he used it.

Moving back to the trailer, he worked on emptying it, finding the rest of his tools like his hammer, tongs, and some pieces of metal to work with. Taking his tools, along with his safety glasses and gloves, he placed everything on the fireplace hearth for now. He left the respirator at the trailer; he was working outside today and didn't think he would need it. As he started placing items back where they belonged, he noticed the temperature starting to rise. The weather people might actually be right and they would enjoy an unseasonably warm day. It might be a good day to have a dinner grill-out.

Done! Putting the last of the items back in the trailer, he looked at his phone. That had taken longer than he had expected. But now he could get to the fun stuff. He double-checked his regulator setting before putting on his safety glasses and a glove on his tong-holding hand. Grabbing the small torch to light the forge, Ian grinned. He couldn't wait to get started. The combination of hammering and the concentration forging required helped get rid of the last of his angst from this morning. He had managed to get two blades made and the pin holes for the handles drilled. Now he just needed to sand them before he could temper. Tempering would take a while, and he was going to confiscate one of the kitchen ovens to do it with. He just needed to make sure any oil was washed off the blades before going in. Running back to his trailer, he grabbed sandpaper, a few wood blocks and a couple of paint sticks. Wrapping the sandpaper around the thin wood would give him a nice sanding tool. Ian also grabbed his blade vice and a clamp. Walking around the picnic table, he attached the vice to the end of the table using the clamp. Rolling up his sleeves, he started sanding the blade and was soon in a rhythm working his way through the different sandpapers. He took the first blade out, checking the smoothness. The edge looked pretty good, but he could see a few scratches still and decided to move to a finer sandpaper to get the finish he wanted. A few minutes later, he wiped it off, happy with how it had turned out. Ian removed it from the vice and placed it off to the side. Standing up he got the second blade secured, making sure there was no wiggle. Bending over to grab the starting sandpaper, he felt lightheaded. He realized that he hadn't eaten since this morning. Standing up all the way took effort, black spots dancing in front of his eyes. He threw out a hand, trying to catch himself on the table. Instead, he felt the sharp edge of his knife slice into his hand and then down his arm as he fell. He didn't even feel his head hitting the ground.

Berkley was closing the cash register as his last customer left. It had been a decent day for sales, which he attributed to the warmer than normal day. Heck, this morning it had been in the twenties, and now it was seventy. It was beautifully sunny too. He heard a sound from outside but couldn't tell what it was. The door slammed open, Shaye running in, her face white and full of fear.

"Let's go," she said, grabbing Berkley's hand.

"What's going on?" Berkley asked, confused. Rolf was standing outside, Tess in the car behind the wheel.

"Give me your keys. I'll lock up and meet you at home," Rolf said, hand out.

"What is going on?" Berkley asked again, this time afraid, blindly giving Rolf his keys.

"Ian," Shaye said, shoving him into the car. "Go, Tess. Hurry."

Pulling through the gates, Berkley's heart was racing. He followed Shaye as she ran to the backyard. His breath caught as he saw Ian crumpled on the ground, blood flowing from his arm. Tess pushed forward, ripping her coat off to press against the gash. Shaye was on her knees next to Ian, pressing one of her hands to his head and holding his injured hand with the other.

"Berkley, try to reach him on the mate bond. Reassure him. If you can rouse him a little bit, try to get him to drink from you. He lost a lot of blood."

'Ian, love. You have to wake up,' Berkley pleaded. *'Wake up*

and drink, please.' He pushed at their bond, trying to get his mate to regain consciousness.

'Ber?' Ian asked weakly.

'Drink. You have to drink,' Berkley told him, placing his wrist at Ian's mouth. He breathed a sigh of relief as he felt Ian's teeth slide into his skin, swallowing what he needed. Shaye sat back a minute later with a smile, letting him know that she had healed Ian's wounds. Rolf came around the corner and helped Berkley move Ian upstairs to their room to get cleaned up.

6

I an woke slowly, enjoying the feel of stretching his arms above his head. His wrist shining in the morning sun. He loved seeing the matching band on Berkley's wrist. It was a collaboration between the two of them; Ian had made the leather bracelets and Berkley had crafted the center stone. It was a gorgeous bead that was spelled against breakage. Ian could feel a few other personal protective spells on it as well. He never took it off, the spell kept the leather safe even in the shower. Rolling on his side, he watched his mate sleep. Berkley was everything he could have asked for in a partner; he was kind, hot as hell, creative, and helped balance Ian's own exuberance.

Berkley had come up with the bracelet idea after Ian had injured himself on the knife blade. It had been deep enough that Ian could have bled out if they hadn't arrived when they did. Berkley wanted to wrap him in bubble wrap and cotton, but that wasn't practical so his mate came up with something Ian could wear that would help protect him from harm. If he had had it when he passed out, he would still have fallen but the bracelet's protections would have stopped him from getting cut. Ian wasn't entirely sure how; if he would have a force field type of thing, if it would have moved him just enough out of the way that he missed the knife. Ian might be the more accident-prone of them but he wanted his Berkley protected as well, so they had made matching bands. They made him smile every time he saw them.

Despite having the love of his life next to him sleeping soundly, Ian's mind was churning. They had a week until their trip. He was excited to see his parents again. They didn't have home internet, so it had been mostly letters and phone calls over the years. His aunt and uncle had given them such a great gift when they turned them, but his parents never really progressed past that time. They had a landline phone and even a truck now, but only because they stood out too much if they brought a horse and wagon into town for supplies. They still tilled the land by animal and by hand, and while his da's newer forge sounded like a thing of beauty, it would not be very modern. Ian was curious to see how much it had changed from the small forge his da' had when he was a kid.

His coming home would also sort of be his coming out. His parents knew in theory that he was gay, but he had never brought anyone home before. All trysts were kept far away from his parents. Once he came to America, he found it was easy enough to find a playmate when he needed one. He never let it get serious, knowing he could have a potential mate out there. His aunt and uncle had been wonderfully supportive when he arrived in the new country. They had set up a plan to establish his background, making sure there would be actual paperwork to support his age and identity, not just the magic and hacking skills of the witch they had hired. When he arrived in the US, he stayed with them at their house, working on what he might want in terms of his new identity. He would be able to use it until his persona was in his nineties or early hundreds with the help of magic. His aunt and uncle really got into their roles of acting as his parents, buying a house in a good school district in a new state. They would all live there for a little while, making sure Ian was registered for school in order to establish a tangible proof of his identity. The witch had already created a birth certificate showing that he was a US citizen having been born abroad, a social security number, and a US passport although he still maintained his separate UK passport for his identity over there. Honestly, he had no idea how the magic worked, but he was glad it did. The plan had been that once he was registered, he could rely on the magic to keep his identity current and updated with college degrees and other things he may need while he traveled and explored his new home.

Aggie and Robert were excited for him to be there, even trying to set him up on some blind dates. Talk about awkward, your "parents" trying to set you up. He knew they were doing it to show their love and acceptance. Once they had moved into the new house, Aggie had hosted an open house to meet the neighbors. It was there that Ian met Shaye, the girl who lived next door. There was just something about the young human that made him change his plans. He decided to stay and suffer through actually attending high school and college instead of leaving like he had originally planned. She had been his best friend, along with Tess and he was so incredibly happy to be with them again. Shaye had always been like a little sister to him, and now they were each other's family under the Clan.

Berkley grumbled in his sleep, reaching out to touch Ian. He always did this right before he woke up. Ian grinned to himself. Lightly tracing a hand down his lover's back, admiring the muscles earned from working with clay all day. Of course, being Fae, he was also naturally stronger and more on the lean side, but his man was certainly fine. Ian rested his hand on the swell of Berkley's ass before lightly smacking it. It had such a great bounce that he did it again to the other cheek.

"It's going to be one of those mornings, is it?" Berkley asked, his voice still rough with sleep, arching his ass up to meet Ian's hand.

"Mmhm," Ian agreed. "Did I tell ye yet this morning that I love ye?"

Berkley laughed. "I just woke up, so no."

"Let me make it up to ye," Ian replied, his eyes twinkling. He disappeared under the sheet.

"Ung," Berkley groaned. "Turn around so I can say good morning too," he begged, hoping Ian would sixty-nine this morning. He had never been a sexual person, but Ian certainly brought it out in him. He knew they didn't have a lot of time before they were supposed to meet the rest of the family downstairs. Ian flipped around, giving Berkley what he asked for.

They were only a few minutes late to the meeting when they tried to sneak into the living room. Shaye glanced up when they entered, eyebrow quirked, shaking her head at them. Berkley was amused to note that she didn't say anything though, probably because her hair was also a little mussed.

Emma cleared her throat. "Now that we're all here," she said, gently teasing them. "We wanted to know if you had decided on what we talked about before."

Berkley looked at Ian, knowing that they had decided to go ahead with the ceremony. In the end, Ian wanted Doc to be comfortable and also to make Berkley happy. What made Berkley happy was having another layer of protection over his mate. Plus, he could tell from Rolf's face that they were a yes as well. Ian would be overjoyed with having his best friend also be immortal.

"Tess and I are a yes," Sam spoke up. Tess nodded.

"Rolf and I are a yes," Shaye added, looking over at Ian. Berkley knew that Ian had finally gotten to talk with Shaye and Tess about Doc's offer. He was glad that his predictions were true.

Gawain looked at Merri. Berkley could tell that they were talking to each other. This was the one couple where he didn't know which way they would go. He could hope they would say yes, but he wasn't sure where they stood. Their faces weren't giving anything away at the moment.

"We're a yes," Merri said quietly. Berkley thought she sounded confident in her answer, but also a little sad. Which he completely understood since the rest of her family were all witches and she would outlive them. She would have anyway, being mated to a falcon shifter, but this guaranteed it.

Berkley and Ian both nodded in agreement. Emma grinned, tears in her eyes as she smiled. Berkley could only imagine what a relief it was that her son wouldn't die before her.

Doc cleared his throat, his eyes also suspiciously blinking. "Thank you, everyone. I can't tell you what this means to us. I, ah. I have everything ready if you wanted to do it now. That gives you guys about a week before you leave to see if it affects you at all," he said to Ian and Berkley.

One by one, the rest of the group nodded. "What do we need to do?" Sam asked.

"I think going outside is probably best for the first part. I'm afraid my animal form might be a tight squeeze in the house. I'll use the Clan link in my human form first, then I'll change to my beast and initiate it in that form. He's a little different," Doc warned them. "He doesn't talk much, mostly single words or short sentences, a lot of pushing of feelings or sensations."

Berkley and Ian followed the group outside.

'Alright, can you all hear me?' Doc asked.

There was a round of affirmations over the telepathic link before Doc took several steps back and changed into his animal form. It still took Berkley's breath away and he had seen it several times now. Doc's alicorn was huge and gorgeous. There was a whinny before they all felt a new presence over the Clan link. *'Mine,'* a voice said smugly.

'Yes, our family,' Emma replied, stroking a hand down his neck.

One by one, each member of the Clan took turns greeting Doc's animal side, making sure to initiate contact over the Clan bond to ensure the first part of the ceremony was complete. It was odd, Berkley thought, Doc and his animal really did seem like separate entities and the animal was not as verbal.

'My tribe,' the animal said before giving the control back to Doc.

Doc changed back to human, taking a moment to listen to himself. "He's finally quiet," he said. "No more 'mine' or pushing to claim you all," he said, laughing. "Next bit will be inside."

Leading the way back into the kitchen, Doc stood by his favorite teapot, the jade one. Berkley watched as he took a knife out of the butcher block. He almost spoke up because there had to be a better way than cutting himself with a knife.

Emma reached out, stilling Doc's hand. "Let's try it another way, huh? One that's a little easier to seal back up."

Doc smiled down at her, love clearly in his eyes, as he held out his wrist. Emma bent over, biting gently, but deeply. As soon as the blood started flowing, she let go and Doc placed his wrist over the teapot. When he deemed that enough was in there, he turned his wrist back over and Emma licked the bites closed. Doc looked at them. "Tess and Berkley already looked over the spell and said it was safe," he reassured them.

Ian watched as Doc held the teapot quietly for a minute before whispering something. He didn't know what the spell was, but he trusted his mate and his friend to know if it would be harmful or not. The teapot seemed to glow as Doc finished.

It wasn't the bright flash of light like when Berkley did a spell, but more of a constant glow, like it was lit from within. Emma grabbed the matching teacups, setting enough out for all of them. Doc poured his blood into each of the cups, it wasn't a lot, about a swallow or two. He accepted his cup, holding it with one hand. He reached out and grabbed Berkley's free hand. He could do this if he was holding his mate, otherwise it still felt like being unfaithful to drink someone else's blood. They were all standing in a circle and raised their glasses at the same time, drinking. Ian thought it tasted a little like grass.

The moment they finished swallowing, Ian could feel a warmth surrounding his body, his arm hairs standing on end like he had touched a staticky surface. The warmth got stronger, his pulse speeding up a bit, and a feeling of euphoria came over him. It reminded him of that singular moment at the peak of climax, where you were chasing the high and finally reached it, that sensation of anticipation finally being realized. But you know, without the sex. His whole body felt buzzed, even after the warmth gradually resided.

Doc looked at them all anxiously. "How do you feel?"

"Like I just had a round of really good sex," Ian admitted, the buzzed feeling loosening his tongue.

Emma snorted, even as Doc looked alarmed. "He's not wrong," she admitted. When Doc looked at her incredulously, she laughed even as she blushed. "It's like when your whole body is striving for the pinnacle and you reach it, right before you fall over. It's like that, but minus any actual orgasms."

Rolf groaned. "Mom," he protested, his cheeks turning red.

"Well, it is," she replied, her own cheeks a little pink.

Ian looked over at Shaye, finding her biting her lip, laughter dancing in her eyes.

"Did it work?" Gawain asked.

"I think so?" Doc replied, pausing for a moment. "My beast says yes."

Emma looked around, a big smile on her face. "Well, I don't feel like cooking and I'm sure you guys don't either, so why don't I order some food and get this cleaned up?"

"That sounds good," Tess agreed.

Berkley took his and Ian's cups over to the sink. "I'll help clean them. We want to make sure to neutralize any blood that might be left so that it doesn't get in the water system or in the wrong hands," he added quietly. He didn't think someone could just take it and become immortal, but he didn't want to take any chances. "I'll run upstairs and get some supplies," he added.

"Thank you," Doc said. "I was wondering about that myself."

"If you need any help, let me know," Tess told Berkley.

It only took him a few minutes to get the things he needed and to cleanse the cups and teapot. He had Tess double-check his work and other than the original blessings on the set, Doc's blood and spell were neutralized and then washed away.

Emma came back in the room. "It seems like everyone is camping out in the living room, when you're done," she said. "I am so glad you both agreed to this. I've just had a nagging feeling lately, but I think this helped it go away."

"What kind of feeling?" Berkley asked. Emma was known for having visions of the future.

She huffed. "That's the most annoying thing. It wasn't like a clear vision, not like it usually is. It was more a feeling of trepidation, of something that was going to happen. There was no vision, no indication of what or who or where. Just this vague feeling. Once the immortality took, the feeling went away, so I can only assume it had something to do with one of us. But it's gone now," she said, relieved. "Just be careful on your trip, okay? I'm happy it's gone, but I hate not knowing what it was about."

When the food arrived, they stayed in the living room, eating on the couches. It felt more like a time to relax and bond, no one wanting to leave the room. Rolf ended up turning on the television and finding a historical documentary to watch. Gawain threw a pepperoni at the screen at the first mistake, leading Sam to grab a bottle of whiskey from the cabinet to have an impromptu Inebriated Inconsistencies night. It had been a while since they had one of these, and the girls hadn't had a chance to attend one yet. Berkley took small sips when the historical gaffes occurred though, knowing there could be many inaccuracies. When the awful documentary ended, they were all completely buzzed, giggling at each other as they stumbled up the stairs to bed. It was a fun night.

7

Berkley stood at the gate, his stomach in knots. He hated flying, something he probably should have told Ian earlier. They were about to leave to see Ian's childhood home, which was something that probably also contributed to him feeling anxious. He had never met anyone's parents before. Berkley hadn't dated much, as he had kept hoping that one day, he would meet his mate. He hadn't wanted to form attachments with someone else, so he had never been in a serious enough relationship to meet the parents.

"Come on, babe. They just called us for seating. What do ye think the seats will be like? I'm looking forward to the extra leg room. I know I hae the window seat, but we can change if you'd like," Ian offered. He could tell Berkley was tense, but he wasn't sure why. He watched as Berkley swallowed hard enough that he could see his throat move. *'What's the matter? Do ye no' want to go?'*

'No, I do. It's stupid. I really hate flying,' Berkley admitted. *'I'm okay once we're up as long as there isn't turbulence, but take-off and landing are bad.'*

Ian took Berkley's hand. *'Is there anything I can do to help?'* He had flown many times, it never bothered him. However, he could tell that Berkley was stressing. Berkley shook his head. Ian kept hold of his hand, leading him into the plane. The first-class seats were spacious, a blanket and pillow already on their seats. He took Berkley's bag and stored it with his own. He tried nudging Berkley to the window seat, but that made him turn even paler. *'No window, please,'* Berkley said.

'Okay, love. I'll sit on the window. I just thought it might help for ye to see out.'

It took a while to get everyone on the plane seated and their bags stored. Their flight attendant had offered them a pre-departure drink, but Ian had turned it down. He asked her to come back once they were in the air; he was afraid Berkley would get sick if he tried drinking now. Ian kept an eye on his mate, trying to send calming vibes across their bond as the stewardess went through the flight safety instructions. Berkley kept his eyes closed and drew in deep breaths as the plane moved. Ian held his hand, rubbing his thumb across the skin, wishing he could do more to help. There was a rumble as the plane lifted off, Berkley squeezing his fingers tight. *'Easy, love. It's okay. Did ye ever join the mile high club? Maybe we can do that during the trip. I could slide into ye, distract ye. Do ye think the bathrooms are any bigger in first class? We may not fit in the regular-sized ones. I could maybe suck ye down as ye lean back against the sink. Or ye could take a 'nap' with a blanket when the lights dim overnight, and I can stroke ye to sleep. What do ye think?'* Ian asked, making sure to draw his words out, letting them sit in the air. He looked at Berkley, finding his shocked gaze on him, his color high and his breathing faster. Looking down, he saw his man was now sporting a semi.

'Ian! You can't make me come in public!' Berkley said, scandalized. He knew he was shyer about PDAs than Ian, but this was a little extreme.

'Well, now you're no' thinking of flying, are ye? Look, we're at height now,' Ian replied smugly.

Berkley glared at his mate as he reached down, trying to discreetly adjust himself. *'Yeah, now I'm just turned on. Blue balls are not fun,'* he complained.

'I'll take care of them later,' Ian promised as the flight attendant came to check on them. He smirked as Berkley quickly dropped a magazine over his lap.

"Could we hae two whiskeys, please?" Ian ordered. "And some pretzels." He figured the drink would help relax Berkley and the pretzels would be bland enough if his stomach was upset from the stress. He kept the blankets close. He fully intended to make Berkley come once everyone was asleep. At least now he knew why Berkley had insisted on flying at night, he must have been planning on sleeping most of the flight away. Ian would just help him fall asleep a little easier.

"Sirs, we're going to land soon," the flight attendant said softly.

Ian woke up, but Berkley was still asleep. "Thank ye," he replied. He quietly packed up their phones and other small things they had sitting out, hoping Berkley would sleep through landing. Berkley had slept sitting up and with his seat belt on, "just in case." There was no big hurry to get off the plane, Ian thought as he mentally went over their next steps. He already had a car booked, they just needed to walk over to the rental office once they collected their bags. He was looking forward to seeing his home country. It had been a while since he had come back to visit. He wanted to have haggis, blood sausage, some curry, and a good old full Scottish breakfast. Ian had booked a hotel room in Oban, which was about a three-hour drive. Tomorrow would hopefully be fun, as he had booked a surprise whiskey distillery tour at the Oban Distillery. He was thinking of adding the whiskey and chocolate event to their tour as well if they had the time. It was by far one of his favorites; the whiskey was smooth, not harsh, or too peaty. Ian planned on buying a few bottles and having them shipped home. He thought they stood a better chance of arriving in one piece if he didn't pack them in his suitcase. He wanted to grab a bottle for his da' as well.

As the plane bumped on the landing, Berkley woke up with a jolt. Ian grabbed his hand, sending calming vibes through their bond.

'It's alright. We're just landing,' Ian reassured him.

'What time is it?' Berkley asked, rubbing his eyes.

'A little before six our time.'

'The sun's up already?' Berkley asked.

'It's six at home but time change, remember? It's eleven here,' Ian responded.

"I thought we would get the car and head into Edinburgh for lunch. There's a pub called The World's End that used to have the best sticky toffee pudding. After we eat, we have about a three-hour drive, depending on traffic," Ian added out loud.

"I didn't know your parents were so close," Berkley replied.

"Nope, no' my parents'. I booked us an overnight. We'll finish driving up to my parents' tomorrow. I wanted to hae a fun night with ye and then I hae something planned for tomorrow afternoon. Then we'll hae another couple hours of driving. We should get to my parents' around dinner time, I would think."

Berkley waited until the seat belt light turned off before standing. He needed a good stretch after sitting for so long. That was probably the best sleep he had had while flying. He was going to attribute it all to Ian being by his side. "Are you going to give me any clues?"

Ian hummed in thought. "I dinnae think so," he replied with a grin, as he stood and gave Berkley a quick kiss. He turned off the airplane mode on his phone to send a quick text to Shaye, letting her know they had landed.

First class had been a nice treat, Ian thought as their bags popped up almost immediately on the baggage carousel. He grabbed his and Berkley's suitcases and they walked over to the rental car station. He had requested a small SUV since you never knew when you would find yourself in a pop-up rainstorm, or maybe even snow since it was February. Both he and Berkley could drive a manual transmission, which gave them more options when it came to car rental in the UK. He read through the paperwork, choosing to get the optional insurance coverage since they weren't in the US, before he and Berkley both signed as designated drivers. Grabbing the keys, he walked out to the car, popping open the trunk for their bags.

"I thought you wanted to drive," Berkley said, looking over the top of the roof.

"I do," Ian replied, looking at him in confusion.

"Well, you might want to switch sides. Different sides of the car and road, remember?" Berkley laughed at him.

"It's been too long since I've been back, I guess. Okay, switch me sides," Ian replied, shaking his head at himself, walking around the car. Starting the car, he chanted to himself, stay on the left, stay on the left, as he pulled out of the lot. His brain quickly remembered how to drive though, and they made it to the pub without any problems.

Finding a parking spot, they walked toward The World's End. Berkley looked around, loving all the old stone buildings, most of which were at least four or five stories high, and the curving roads that were a mix of cobblestone and blacktop. It made him feel comfortable, the age of the town reminding him of when he was younger, how cities weren't always built in a grid pattern. There was something that seemed more welcoming, warmer, and familiar about a town that kind of meandered along without a set plan. Walking along the dark gray granite sidewalks, they reached their destination. The blue paint and gold letters on the front of the pub were certainly eye-catching against the grayish brown of the stone around it. Standing just inside the doorway, they took a minute to allow their eyes to adjust to the dimmer lighting. The pub was small, cozy, and Ian could smell all the delicious foods coming from the kitchen. He loved the bare stone walls and the knickknacks decorating the place. They were lucky enough to find a seat at a table. Ian looked at the menu, even though he knew what he was going to get. He always got the fish and chips.

"What can I get ye today?" their waitress asked when she came over.

"Could we get two waters? For an appetizer, I'd like to start wi' an order of haggis fritters and I'll hae the fish and chips."

"I'll have the steak and ale pie," Berkley added. "Could we get the sticky toffee pudding when the fritters come out as well?"

"Ye do love me." Ian grinned as she walked away to put in their order.

"If you fill up on fish and chips, you're going to be upset if you miss dessert. You've talked about it enough," Berkley teased.

About ten minutes later their dessert and appetizer arrived.

Ian scooped a bite of the pudding and fed it to Berkley.

"Hm, that is good," Berkley said.

Ian squirmed in his seat, watching as Berkley's tongue licked a drop of sauce from his lips. He reached down to quickly adjust himself. *'Stop eating like that,'* he demanded. *'I cannae take care of this here and we hae three hours in the car until we get to the hotel.'*

Berkley grinned widely. *'Maybe one day we can stay in bed, with just some sauce to keep us company…'*

'*That's no' helping,*' Ian responded firmly before looking down at the table. He tried to think of unsexy things to help his erection go down. Walking in that time to find his aunt and uncle having sex, his parents having sex. He breathed out as his erection finally died with those images. He took a large bite of the pudding, letting out a small groan at the taste. He could never replicate the sticky toffee pudding when he tried to make it. It turned out okay, but never as good as this one.

Their main courses came out and everything was as delicious as he remembered it to be. The fried fish was so large that the ends were hanging off the plate. He shared a few bites of his fish and tried the steak pie in return. They settled the check and headed back out into the sunshine. Ian wanted to grab a cup of coffee from the nearby café before leaving. When he saw a souvenir shop nearby, he pulled Berkley in. Ian was now on a mission. While Berkley browsed, Ian snuck into the bathroom. He was hoping that the naughty vending machine was still here. He started laughing when he saw the new selections. Oh! The blow-up sheep was in stock! He would have to break that out sometime on the drive, he thought as he purchased it. Not that they would *use* the nice lady sheep, but he thought it would be funny to see how red his partner could get. Berkley was somehow older than he was but more reserved and less experienced when it came to sex. If he had to guess, he would say Berkley fell somewhere on the demisexual spectrum. It certainly was fun introducing him to new things. He looked at the machine again, before deciding to buy some of the individual packets of lube. He just couldn't imagine getting intimate with Berkley under his parents' roof; their two-bed house wasn't very big or soundproof. He planned on sneaking off somewhere on his parents' property to spend time with Berkley. He removed the plastic blow-up sheep from its packaging and stuffed it in his coat pocket, along with the packets.

He stepped out of the bathroom, spotting Berkley talking with the cashier.

"What did ye find?" he asked, placing a hand on Berkley's lower back.

"I wanted to grab a postcard to send home and was asking if they sold stamps here," Berkley replied, addressing the card.

"I'm sure the girls will love it," Ian responded. He remembered Shaye getting excited when anyone would send physical mail to the apartment. She always got such a kick out of it.

The cashier said she would drop the postcard in the mail for them, which was nice. They headed back to the car, this time Ian remembering to go to the right...err, left side.

"We have about three, three and half hours before getting to our next stop. Feel free to take a quick nap if ye want to, or I hae a playlist I put on my phone for the trip," Ian told him.

"Let's start with the playlist. I may sleep after eating all that food, but I'm good right now," Berkley replied.

It was a nice drive, the day staying at least partly sunny, no rain or snow yet, and traffic wasn't too heavy. They made decent time to the hotel, which faced the water and wasn't far from their outing tomorrow.

"Oh, this is cute," Berkley said, as they walked to the front of the hotel. The front was made of large stone bricks, with various depths to the façade. There were bay windows, a small turret, and two of the top windows had a castle look with a stone balcony railing. The front entrance to the hotel jutted out next to a patio. The entryway was topped with a stone railing; Berkley couldn't tell from standing on the street if it was decorative or if it was also used as an outdoor space. The patio to the left of the entrance was smaller, but it would be an amazing place to sit during warmer months and people-watch or look out over the water. They were lucky that they had found nearby parking and didn't have to drag their luggage very far. He guessed that was one of the benefits of vacationing during the non-peak season. Ian went to check in while Berkley looked around the lobby.

"Ber, did ye want to go to the restaurant here? It's Mediterranean type of food. They recommend reservations, I could get us in around seven or eight tonight; that should give us time to walk around a wee bit and explore. What do ye think?" Ian asked from the front desk.

"Hm, let's do eight, just to make sure we have enough time," Berkley replied. The town looked amazing, but he also wanted to have some time with Ian in their room.

"Here are your room keys. I have your dinner reservation secured. If you need any help with places to visit or need anything for your room, please let me know," the front desk concierge told them. "We also have the lounge, if you are interested in drinks later. The spa is open as well, you would call down to book a session."

Ian thanked her and they headed to their room. Berkley's breath caught as he stepped over the threshold. It was bright and airy, the walls painted in a light cream and shades of blue. There was a king-sized bed with a small bench seat at the end, a small table and two chairs overlooking an amazing view of the water. He could easily see them having a coffee or a tea in the morning, watching the sun come up.

"I booked us a suite wi' the sea view," Ian said, wrapping his arms around Berkley's waist from behind. "I thought it would be a nice treat."

"It's amazing. I love the view, thank you." He leaned back against Ian's chest, loving how warm and safe being held like this made him feel. They watched the birds glide by and the boats out on the water for a few minutes before unpacking a few clothes for dinner and setting their toiletries in the bathroom. "This bathroom is nice. Most hotel bathrooms are so small." The double sinks were a nice luxury that not every hotel had. Berkley laid his toothbrush and comb by one of the sinks, Ian doing the same at the other. Berkley loved having two sinks; Ian's side was normally messier than his.

"As much as I would love to stay in here with ye, we should probably head out. Wi' it being the off season, I'm no' sure how late everything is open," Ian said, grabbing a handful of Berkley's butt.

Berkley heaved a sigh, turning his head for a kiss. "Let's go then. I heard good things about the local distillery," he said, turning just in time to see Ian try to hide a smile. "What?" he asked suspiciously.

"That's my surprise for tomorrow. Surprise! We hae a distillery tour at one thirty."

Berkley smiled, that did sound fun. "Let's see what else we can find in town then. Should I be looking for souvenirs, or wait until we are at your parents'?" He wasn't sure how rural Ian's parents' home was.

"There's a few small towns nearby, within a half hour to an hour drive, but if we see something we like here, we should get it," Ian answered.

Ian grabbed his hand and pulled him in for a kiss.

Walking out of the hotel, they turned to the right, heading toward the distillery. It had looked like there were several shops down that way. They walked slowly, just enjoying being able to stretch their legs. A window display caught Ian's eye.

"What are you looking at?" Berkley asked, confused.

"Purses," Ian replied.

"Okay…" Berkley drew out. He had never seen Ian with a purse, his sporran sometimes if he was in his kilt, but never a purse.

"For one of the girls," Ian responded, elbowing his mate in the side. He could pick one out for each of them, but he wasn't sure if that was the right gift.

"We can always come back tonight or tomorrow if you don't see anything else. If you're thinking for each of them, that could take up a fair amount of room in the suitcases," Berkley pointed out. Not that it really mattered, they could see how much it would cost to mail or pick up a small suitcase to keep the souvenirs in.

"That's a good idea. Let's keep looking," Ian replied, giving the bags one last look.

A little farther down they stopped at a coffee shop, enjoying the smell as they walked through the door. Working their way down the street with their new cups of coffee, they explored the soap shop, where Ian did buy a few soaps that he thought Emma would like. Berkley grabbed a couple postcards from a souvenir shop.

"You just sent one this morning. Are ye sending another one?" Ian asked.

Berkley shrugged. "Maybe. I like to grab a postcard from places I've been, it's something small to keep. I have a book I keep them in at home. Sometimes I'll write notes about what I did there on the back. When I was traveling, I liked to have mementos, but didn't want to lug around heavy things." He felt his face get a little pink.

"Where's this book? I haven't seen it!" They had been living together almost three months and he couldn't remember seeing that type of book.

"It's on one of the bookcases. It looks like a binder," Berkley replied.

"You'll hae to show it to me when we get home," Ian said. "I would love to see all the places ye've been. I get keychains or small ornaments. I tried stickers on my trailer for a while. I had them on the inside wall to keep them safe and also not to draw more attention to myself. I was pissed when someone damaged the trailer and I had to get a new one. The stickers aren't made to be transferred over, so I went back to the keychains and ornaments. I think I hae them in a box in the basement. Before that I would get wee knickknacks or something I found that would remind me, like a special rock or shell."

"I like the keychain idea; that's another good small souvenir," Berkley replied. It would be fun to compare the places they had been. When he got out his postcards, he would have Ian grab his box as well. He reached out and grabbed Ian's hand for a quick squeeze. They were going to stop and get an ice cream, but Ian saw a chocolate shop that he wanted to check out. Stepping inside, Berkley watched as Ian stood there, eyes closed, breathing in the scent of chocolate. His mate had a bit of a sweet tooth. "Let's go," he said, poking Ian into moving from blocking the doorway. "We can grab some to enjoy after dinner," he suggested.

Ian browsed the glass display, looking at all the delicious-looking chocolates. When an employee walked by, he stopped them. "Excuse me. Do ye send internationally?" he asked. He thought the family would get a kick out of some of these flavors.

"We do," the young man answered.

"Great! I'd like to do a box of thirty-six to mail, and then a box of twenty-four and a box of sixteen for takeaway," Ian replied. He'd bring his mam a box, keep a box for himself and Berkley, and mail the bigger box home. Thirty-six should be enough for them to share. "For the large box, I would like four of the dark coffee creams, six of the whiskey truffles, three sticky toffee puddings, two apple crumble truffles, two hazelnut and caramel..."

Berkley spoke up. "One of the caramelized banana and rum cup, one strawberry and balsamic cream. I think Sam would like those," he told Ian.

"What else do ye think?" Ian asked.

"Let's get two marmite chocolates, they can cut it, and each try a bite. It sounds a little gross honestly; I'm not a marmite fan. Maybe then fill it with their most popular flavors?" Berkley suggested.

"That sounds good. Think about the ones ye want for our box," Ian told him before finishing the order for the box to mail back home. While Ian went with the employee to deal with the shipping details, another employee came over and Berkley picked out their chocolates.

"Ian, I finished our box. What do you want for your mom's?" Berkley asked.

"Hold on, I'm coming," Ian replied, finishing writing a note to put in with the box of chocolates for the Clan. "Mam is very picky about her flavors, she's no' very adventurous," he explained. He picked out a mix of some dark, milk, and a couple white chocolates. Most of the fillings he chose were caramel or fruit flavors, definitely no marmite or chili. After paying and taking the two boxes to go, they headed down the street, stopping in front of the War & Peace Museum.

"It says closed until March. Maybe we could make a stop if we ever come back with the whole family. It looks like it could be interesting. It's crazy that it's free, they just take donations," Ian said.

"I bet the guys would love it," Berkley said aloud. *'I think most of us were in the US during the last war, so I don't know that we would be able to play Inebriated Inconsistencies quite as well with the museum,'* he finished telepathically.

'I'm pretty sure they don't allow shots of alcohol in any museum,' Ian replied dryly with a smile.

'Probably not,' Berkley agreed.

Walking along the waterfront, they paused to look at the sea. The low tide was almost at its peak, and it was amazing to see boats tied up and resting on the mud until the water came back in. They kept walking toward their hotel, taking a slight detour to stop at a bookshop. It was fun browsing and seeing what the different offerings were.

Ian looked down at his watch. "We better get going so we can hae enough time to get changed before dinner." They had plenty of time still, but he was hoping to sneak in some quality time with Berkley.

Berkley looked at him and raised an eyebrow when he saw they easily had thirty to forty-five minutes left and their hotel was a minute away. "Sure," he agreed, smirking at Ian. He had an idea of what his mate wanted to do.

Heading into the hotel, they took the stairs up to their room. Berkley looked over his shoulder and saw his mate staring at his arse. He cleared his throat and put on an affronted face. "Excuse me, may I help you with something?" he said primly, his cock twitching behind his zipper.

"Hm, possibly. I was thinking of getting a shower. Ye could help scrub my back?" Ian replied in a serious tone, although his lips were twitching like he wanted to smile.

"It's an intriguing offer. What could you offer me for such a service?" Berkley questioned, playing along.

"I could scrub your back as well?" Ian offered questioningly.

"Are you any good at back washing? I have very high standards," he replied loftily, biting the inside of his cheek to keep from laughing.

"Aye, I think ye will be pleased," Ian replied.

Ian sped up the last couple of stairs to reach Berkley. Tangling his hands in that gorgeous silvery hair, he held his mate's face. *'I love ye, my Fae,'* Ian said as he kissed Berkley. He pushed him up against the wall, leaning his body into Berkley's, tongues rubbing together. Ian groaned at the feel of Berkley's cock filling. Berkley reached down, hooking his thumbs in Ian's back belt loops, sliding under his shirt and caressing the skin. Ian pressed his groin against Berkley's, causing them both to gasp.

'Let's go to our room,' Berkley said, pulling Ian by his waistband. As hot as this was, he didn't want to get arrested for public indecency.

Ian stumbled through the door, slamming it shut as soon

as they were in. He dragged his mate through the room with him, kissing and stripping on the way. By the time they made it the relatively short distance to the bathroom, they were only in their underwear. Berkley fumbled behind him, searching for the knob to turn on the shower. The bathroom soon filled with steam and Ian pushed Berkley under the water, grabbing the lube they had left there earlier.

8

The drive went a lot faster than it did when he was by himself. It was nice having a traveling companion, Ian mused as he drove to his parents' home. Eventually it became more rural, the buildings and towns spreading out. Ian loved watching Berkley's face as they started passing fields scattered with sheep and Highland cattle. The landscape soothed something in him, seeing his first home again. The reds, greens, and browns painting the landscape, little streams and waterfalls popping out of nowhere. He loved seeing all the short stone walls and the remains of stone structures dotting the landscape. As the road narrowed, he had to pull into the mud a bit because a cow was walking down the road. He slowed down, not wanting to hit the animal, which allowed Berkley to roll down his window so he could say hi to the cow. Ian could have told him that was a bad idea.

"Hello, cow," Berkley said politely. "You would be safer off the road."

Ian started laughing as the smell started to hit Berkley's nose. He grabbed his phone in a hurry to snap a picture to send to the group back home.

"What is that smell? Oh my god," Berkley exclaimed, rolling the window up in a hurry.

"Yeah, they look all cute and shaggy, but they can really smell when they're covered in mud like she is," Ian told his mate with a grin.

"Why?"

"I'm no' sure. I just know that when I'm near one that is as muddy as that one, chances are it's going to smell. Maybe it's a combination of mud, bog, peat, possibly even manure. Now, if ye come across one that doesn't look like it's been rolling in the mud, then they don't smell bad," Ian added as he pulled away from the cow and started driving faster. "We're getting closer. I'm going to stop to get gas in the next town and then we hae about thirty minutes after that. It gets to be a one-lane road right near my parents' land." They drove for a little longer, listening to music on the playlist Ian had created for the trip. The gas station was small, only two pumps, but they were the only ones there, so they didn't have to wait.

Berkley jumped out first, claiming that Ian was driving so he would fill up the tank. When he was done pumping the gas, he ran inside to grab them each a drink and a snack. Lunch had been amazing again, but he knew that Ian would be getting hungry soon.

Climbing back in the car, he passed Ian a trail mix and a soda. "I have some beef jerky and cookies too," he told Ian. "I forgot that gas is in liters here, not gallons. It's bloody expensive!"

"The SUV probably doesn't help us there, but I figured it would be better to hae it in case we need the extra power. Mam and Da's drive can be a little muddy this time of year. I made the mistake of renting a compact car one year and it took all three of us to get it unstuck and pushed down the road enough where I could get on the paved section. It was a mess. Thank ye for my snack," Ian said, leaning over to give Berkley a kiss on the cheek.

Berkley smiled back, giving Ian's hand a squeeze before letting go so Ian could shift the car into gear. He sang along to the song that came on and watched the scenery. It was pretty here, though it was a little overcast and he thought they might get a bit of rain or snow today. He loved seeing all the little waterfalls. The colors were gorgeous too, not in your face bright, but the greens, tans, and reds of the hillside was eye-catching. He should see if he could find a painting or a photograph to hang in their home. He bet Ian would like to see part of his homeland, and it would make a great visual. At the moment, their room back home was a little bare. He thought that they were each hesitant to put too much of their own stuff out, not wanting the other to feel like they were taking over the space. The artwork would be something that they both would enjoy, he thought. They really needed to take the time to go through all their boxes and belongings and figure out how to decorate their space so that it reflected both of them.

About twenty minutes later they drove through a little village. The main town was tiny with a small convenience store-slash-post office, based on the sign out front, and a lot of small homes.

"This is the village," Ian said. "When Mam and Da' need farm supplies, they need to go a little further out, or sometimes Bert will order it in for them and they pick it up here. There's no' much to it and most of the people who stay here are older, the younger ones tend to leave to find bigger towns. It's slightly bigger than when I lived here, but no' by much. The people are generally nice though, sometimes a little standoffish if you're no' from around here. The farm is a few more minutes out and then we'll get to see just how good the driveway is. I've offered to get it paved for them, but they refuse to update it. Two years ago, I ordered a load of gravel to be delivered and had it spread as their Christmas present, so hopefully it won't be too bad," Ian said.

Berkley could feel Ian stressing through their bond. He had already been prepared that the house was a simple two-bed, one-bathroom house heated by the wood stove and a fireplace. Ian's parents used a minimal amount electricity and only had a landline telephone. Ian had installed both of those updates to the house during previous visits, mostly so he could use the telephone to keep in contact with his parents and have hot water and indoor plumbing when he came to visit.

"Babe, it will be fine. I have no great expectations. Remember I'm older than you; I've lived without the nicer amenities for much longer than I've had them. You've prepared me for it to be rougher, for your parents to be reserved and awkward. It's important to you that I meet them, so that's what we're going to do. It will be fine. We're fated, nothing else matters. We have our family at home who love us no matter what. Now, stop the car, give me a kiss, and take a deep breath," Berkley instructed.

Ian looked at him out of the corner of his eye, but he pulled the car over. "I know I'm being ridiculous. I told them years ago I was gay, but I never brought anyone near them so they just kind of ignored it. I dinnae want them to hurt your feelings."

"Look at me," Berkley said firmly. Ian was normally so confident in everything he did that this was quite a change. "I don't know them. They're not my family or my friends. They don't have the power to hurt me. The only thing they could do to upset me would be to hurt you. *That* would hurt me. If they don't like me, that sucks, but we don't live here, and I can deal with it until we go home. We have our family at home that loves us unconditionally. You have your aunt and uncle, I have my family. My family is definitely a love-but-don't-show-it-well, reserved family, which you'll see when you meet them. Most of the Fae are, but my point is I am not expecting warm hugs or lots of affection. This is a fun trip for us to see your homeland and to introduce me. Everything else that is positive is just a happy bonus. It will be fine," Berkley said firmly, leaning over to lightly kiss Ian.

"Thank ye, love," Ian replied softly. He wasn't really sure how his parents would react, although they seemed okay when they met Berkley over the phone. He reached out, cupping Berkley's cheek and giving him another soft kiss.

"Let's get to it then," Berkley said with a smile.

Ian put the car back into gear, heading out of town to the long driveway that led to his parents' farm. He breathed a small sigh of relief to himself when it looked relatively intact. The gravel was still in place. He had paid a small fortune to make sure it had a thick base to last a while and he was glad to see it had worked. There were a few small ruts, but it wasn't bad at all. He pulled up to the rectangular house, putting the car in park and taking a deep breath.

Berkley reached over to squeeze his hand before getting out of the car and stretching. He stood looking at the house. It was a cute home; the single-story rectangular stone building held a chimney stack at either end, both of which had smoke lazily drifting out. The front door was right in the middle of the house, a window located on either side. The roof looked like slate and had two dormer windows, which from here he couldn't tell if they were simply for light or if there was a loft area. Berkley looked around the farm, noticing a few outbuildings. It looked like there was a woodshed, a barn, and what was probably the forge.

Ian turned the car off and sent a quick text to the group letting them know they had arrived, before getting out and walking toward the back to get their luggage. The sky opened up as soon as he reached for the hatch handle, pelting them with hail and snow. "Ow, shite," Ian said, grabbing Berkley's hand and pulling him to stand under the porch roof. "I dinnae miss the random pop-up hailstorms," he muttered, watching the pellets bounce off the ground.

The front door creaked open, his mam poking her head out. "Is it snowing?" she asked.

"Yeah, Mam. It just started," Ian replied, his brogue deepening as he spoke to her. Berkley licked his lips but had to focus on not getting an erection in front of his new mother-in-law. That was not the first impression he wanted to make. He would just have to ask Ian to talk like that when they were alone. Ian moved to the side, putting his hand against the small of Berkley's back. "Mam, this is my mate Berkley. Berkley, this is my mam, Charlotte," he said nervously.

His mam nodded her head in greeting. "Nice to meet ye," she replied. "Come on in, ye can get your bags when this nonsense has stopped," she instructed before turning to go back into the house.

'*Okay then,*' Ian said.

'*Let's go in,*' Berkley encouraged. It was a little bit chilly with the hail and snow coming down.

Wiping their feet on the doormat, they walked inside. Berkley looked around curiously. The floors were stone with some woven rugs strewn about. Straight ahead was a large sized L-shaped sofa. Looking to his right, there was a square table and chair set with just enough room for four people. The shorter length wall held a large hearth in the middle, where the original fireplace must have been. It had been converted to house a large wood-burning stove, where Ian's mom stood heating water for tea. To the right of the fireplace, a refrigerator stood in the corner, the sink and a small countertop sitting under the front window. To the left of the stove stood a traditional box bed. A custom-built armoire had been built into the end of it. Looking to his left, Berkley saw a coat stand, where he placed his coat and held his hand out for Ian's to hang up as well. There was another fireplace at this end, this one still being used as a traditional fireplace, a small fire burning to keep the room warm. There was another box bed and armoire in the back left corner. The entire layout was one large open room, except for an enclosed area located in the front left corner of the house. Based on what Berkley could remember of homes this old, the internal walls must have been added sometime after the house was built.

'That's the bathroom,' Ian told Berkley, nodding toward the enclosed space.

"I figured you'll share a bed?" she questioned, staring down at the kettle as if to make it boil faster.

"Aye," Ian replied simply.

She nodded once. "I put fresh sheets on this morning and towels in your dresser. Your da' took the wagon to get some more firewood, but he should be back soon. Ye can hae a seat, the tea should be ready soon."

"Does he need any help? We can go out and load it up," Berkley offered.

"Nae, he should be about done. Maybe when he gets back, ye can help stack?" she replied.

"Sure," Ian said. The silence that followed was just as awkward as he imagined.

'At least she isn't fighting us sharing a room,' Berkley pointed out.

'There are only two beds. And I wouldna call it a room. It's just a box bed,' Ian pointed out dryly.

'There's always the couch or the floor,' Berkley responded.

Berkley wasn't sure how he ended up in a situation where it seemed like he was going to be the talkative one in the group, when it was normally Ian running the conversations. Which totally suited Berkley; however, today it seemed that Ian was being the quiet one.

"Did Ian tell you all about the house we all live in now?" Berkley asked, trying to think of something that could be a longer conversation and draw both of them into talking.

"No' much, just that his friend mated and that the house was large enough for all of ye and formed a Clan of sorts."

Berkley nodded. "Rolf has a lot of land and a large house.

It backs up into the National Park, so there is a lot of privacy. When Rolf and Shaye mated, they invited us all to live in the house and form the Clan. All of us have found our mates, which is amazing. They're a good group of people. We have a large range of ages and professions. Doc is…well, a doctor, Emma knits and has her own small farm in England. Merri is a librarian, and her mate Gawain is a historian. Sam owns the brewery and restaurant in town. Tess and Shaye are nurses. Rolf handles investments."

"What do ye do?" she asked.

"Let me run out to the car, I'll be right back," Berkley said, rushing out the door to grab his carry-on. Back inside, he placed his bag on a chair and started digging through it before pulling out a box. "This is for you," he said, handing it to Ian's mom. "I made this before we left." Hopefully it was packed well enough to survive the travel.

"Oh! Thank ye," she said with a slight blush. She poured the boiling water into the teapot before sitting down to open the gift. Pulling out something wrapped in tissue and bubble wrap, she finally revealed a tall thin vase with various shades of blue in the glaze. "It's lovely, thank ye. Ye made this?"

Berkley nodded. "I'm a potter. I have a shop in town, and I also sell things online."

Charlotte looked at her son. "Ye are still blacksmithing?"

"Aye, and leatherworking. I'm working out of Berkley's old apartment and in the backyard at the house right now. Ber's made space in his displays to sell some of my items. Berkley's store is in a great location and the shop that shares a wall on the left is thinking of selling; if they do, we'd buy it and knock down part of the shared wall to make it into one larger shop, or at least hae a large open doorway connecting our two spaces. Berkley would hae his original space and I would take over the new side. My side would be for the leather goods and finished knives or swords, bracelets, that type of thing. Rolf is letting us build a workshop on the property. I wanted to see Da's forge and get some ideas. We hae no' been able to come up with a finished plan yet. I want to start building it in the spring when the ground is thawed and it's a little warmer," Ian replied.

"That sounds nice," his mom replied. "Your da' has been mostly using the forge to shoe the horses, but I'm sure he will love to tell ye about it. Are the people ye live wi' mostly paranormals? Shaye's human, if I remember?"

"She was," Ian confirmed. "She's a vampire now; she turned back in November. Tess and Merri are sisters, both witches. Sam is a werewolf, Doc and Gawain are shifters, Emma is Rolf's mam and a vampire. Berkley is Fae," Ian told his mam.

"That's. That's a range," Charlotte said hesitantly. She hadn't met very many other paranormals. They stayed close to their farm for the most part and their town was small enough that they didn't get many travelers through.

"Aye. We hae a huge age range too. The newest member is only a couple of weeks old," Ian replied, pulling out his phone.

"Did someone hae a bairn?"

"Nae. Emma adopted a little wolf-dog pup that had been orphaned. Here's a picture," Ian replied, showing his mam the phone.

"Oh he's wee. Cute though."

Berkley nodded. "We've all been taking turns feeding him and taking him outside. He still doesn't have a name yet. They wanted to wait until his personality started to show a little bit."

They heard clomping on the front porch and the door swung open.

"Charlotte, who's here?" Ian's dad, James, called out from the porch as he bent over to remove his boots.

"Ian and his mate Berkley arrived," she replied.

Ian's dad looked up. Berkley could see some of Ian's

features in his father. His dad had darker hair, more of a brown with red highlights, but Ian must have inherited the freckles from him. Their noses were similar as well. His dad was about the same height, whereas his mom was much shorter. "Urm. Afternoon. How was the drive?" he asked gruffly.

"It was good. It was uneventful until we got to the house and the hail hit. Da', this is my mate Berkley, Berkley this is my da', James," Ian introduced them as Ian's dad came over to stand by his wife at the table.

Berkley stood, offering his hand. "It's nice to meet you," he said.

"Aye, ye as weel," James replied.

Charlotte stood up, getting another cup down for tea.

"Da', did ye need any help stacking the wood? Ber and I can help," Ian offered.

"Ah, sure," James said. "It's no' a lot, just a wagonful."

"Go on then," Charlotte shooed them out. "I'll put a new pot of tea on for when you're done."

Grabbing their coats, they followed James out the door. The wagon was hooked up to a larger-sized workhorse and was stuffed full of chopped wood. The porch held a large wood rack on the far end. Working together, they filled the rack next to the house before guiding the horse and wagon to the storage shed to drop off the rest of the wood. It made Ian happy to see his partner and da' working together, even if there wasn't a lot of talking going on. The atmosphere felt like there was an uneasy truce, even though there had been no fighting. It was more that it was an awkward silence, it being difficult to connect to each other. Frankly, it was going better than Ian had expected. He had never brought anyone home before and it surprised him that they were being as open as they were with meeting Berkley.

"That should do it," James said as they placed the last few

logs. "Let me get Mo here put away and we can go get some of your mam's tea."

They followed him to the barn, where James unhooked the wagon. It was set back from the house, between the house and the woodshed. There was a fenced-in area along the backside of the barn that probably connected to a back door. From his limited view of the fenced area, Berkley could see a pair of cows, a donkey, and a few large pigs hanging out, grazing in the pen. He could hear clucking coming from somewhere, so there must be a chicken coop as well. Walking inside the barn, Berkley chuckled as several heads poked over stall doors when they heard them enter. A few horses whinnied a greeting, and he walked over to say hello and stroke their noses.

'Making friends already, I see,' Ian teased as he walked over to help his da' remove the harness from the horse.

'Perks of being Fae,' Berkley replied. He had no idea why, but animals seemed to like the Fae.

"Huh," James grunted as he came over after brushing down and getting the stall ready for Mo. "Gertie never likes anybody. She normally tries to take a bite out of anyone that comes near her."

"She's a good girl," Berkley protested. "Just a little feisty," he added as he scratched down her neck, earning himself a nuzzle.

Ian smiled, knowing that if the animals liked Berkley, his da' would be more open to him. He trusted the animals and their instincts. Having the orneriest animal there love on Berkley could only help his da' like him more. Walking back toward the doors, they stopped to wash their hands at the pump. They waited until his da' shut and secured the barn doors before walking to the house. Ian could smell something baking under the smell of wood smoke coming from the chimney. He hoped it was his mam's scones. She made a great clotted cream to go with them and he hadn't had them in a long time.

"Wash your hands," Charlotte told them. "The scones are just about ready."

"We already did," James said.

"Good. Ian, can ye grab the clotted cream out of the refrigerator?"

"Sure, Mam. I can't wait to hae some. Ye make the best scones and cream."

'She makes the best cream, huh,' Berkley teased him.

'Shut up! Ew. That's not what I meant,' Ian replied. *'Don't make me tell Mam ye don't want any,'* Ian threatened.

'I'll be quiet,' Berkley replied, laughing.

"Can I help with anything?" Berkley asked.

"Can ye take some plates out? They're in that cabinet." Charlotte pointed it out.

Berkley nodded and moved to take out four plates. "Do you want them here, or at the table?"

"Table please," she replied as she bent down to take the scones out of the wood-powered stove. As the door opened, the mouthwatering smell of fresh-baked scones wafted out. James pulled open a drawer and took out some knives and napkins.

Berkley waited until Charlotte and James took a scone before serving Ian and himself. Cutting the scone in half, the knife passed through easily, a few crumbs falling to the plate. The clotted cream was perfectly salted and melted on the hot scone. Taking a bite, he let out a quiet moan. He finished his bite, licking his lips to get the cream clinging to them. Looking up, he saw everyone staring at him. Berkley felt his cheeks turn red.

"These are delicious! Thank you for making them," Berkley said. He glanced at Ian. "You know who would love these?"

"Shaye," they said together.

"That's your friend from when ye lived wi' your aunt and uncle?" James asked.

Ian nodded. "She's more like a sister. She's married, well mated, to Rolf. They haven't set a wedding date yet. She loves bread, any kind really," Ian replied.

"Are they getting married then?" Charlotte asked.

Ian nodded. "They got engaged on her birthday. Rolf wanted her to feel loved in both human and paranormal worlds. It's been a little crazy lately and they haven't finalized a date yet."

"Ye didn't mention much about what happened the past few months. What's been going on?" James asked.

Ian looked at Berkley, who gave him a tiny shrug. He hadn't told his parents much about what had happened because he knew they would worry. His mam might have even brought up moving back home or to find someplace "safer" to live. It had been a frequent argument in the beginning when he started exploring outside of his small town. He sighed. If he was ever going to bring the whole group to visit, someone was bound to say something, so it was better to just let it out now.

"Mam, ye might want more tea for this," Ian recommended, waiting until his mother made a new pot of tea and set it in the middle of the table. "It's a wee bit of a story, but I'll try to make it quick. Uh, where to start? Ye're going to ken some of this, but it all adds together so stick with me. Okay, so I met Shaye when I enrolled in the high school with Aunt and Uncle. There was something about her that drew me in, dinnae ken what but I just knew we were going to be friends. It's why I stayed there. Her parents were shite, they ignored her because she had a healing gift that wasn't 'natural' according to them. Never mind that she only tried to help people...anyway," Ian stopped his rant before it started. "When she chose LSU for college, I went wi' her. It's always fun to learn. I chose a business major since I wanted to get more serious about making my leather and blacksmithing into a full-time career. I had sold things as I traveled, but if I could set up an online shop or book my services with festivals, I'd have a steadier income.

"We met Tess in New Orleans. She's a witch and was there visiting family. She decided to find a job and stay there as well. We became a trio, we hung out all the time. Neither of us told Shaye about paranormals, which we both hated because we knew about her gifts. When Shaye graduated and left NOLA, I started taking more travel gigs. We still talked on the phone and texted, but it wasn't the same. She really does feel like my little sister, and I hated that I wasn't supposed to tell her the truth about myself. Her last assignment was in Rockfort, where she met Rolf and saved his life. His father was Vlad, I'm no' sure if you've heard of him?" Ian paused in his story to look at his parents.

"I think Aggie mentioned him at one time?" Charlotte said questioningly, looking at James.

"Aye, think so," James confirmed.

"He was bad news. Power hungry, thought vampires were the superior being, loved hurting people just for fun. He was Rolf's da'. He…" Ian stopped for a second, not wanting to say too much about Emma's history but it was a big part of the story. "Attacked Emma many years ago when she was human, and Rolf was born nine months later. He was trying to create successors or something, not entirely sure of his reasoning. Vlad turned Rolf without his consent when he was twenty-five and tried to sway Rolf to his side. When he couldn't, Vlad eventually attacked him. Shaye saved Rolf and her whole world was blown open when she learned about mates and paranormals. Vlad used someone to poison Rolf's blood supply, but Shaye and the family were able to save him again. They decided to set up a trap to lure Vlad in and stop the attacks for good.

"I hadn't heard about any of this since I was traveling

with a Renaissance group at the time that was mostly human. Shaye called once Tess spilled that she was a witch, and I was a vampire. I told them I was coming to help with the fight. Shaye turned so that she would be stronger and harder to kill. On the plus side, her gifts became easier to control and she wasn't drained nearly as quickly as when she had been human. Emma came in from her home in England, Gawain came in from… I don't actually ken where he was. Do you?" Ian asked Berkley.

Berkley shook his head. "I don't know that he ever said."

Ian shrugged before continuing. "I had some delays when I ran into a group of Vlad's minions, but I managed to arrive the morning of the fight. That was when I met Berkley," Ian added with a smile. He grabbed Berkley's hand, raising it to kiss the palm. "I unloaded the gear and weapons I had brought to help, and we had some time left before the plan was supposed to be enacted and were able to claim each other. Vlad fell for the trap and although Rolf tried to give him one more chance, he still attacked and was eventually defeated. Some of his followers were killed, some ran away. This was mid-November and we thought we were done.

"After Thanksgiving, Sam and Tess went to visit her family—" Ian continued.

"Wait a second. Who's Sam?" James asked, confused. He was having a hard time keeping people straight.

"Sam is the owner of the brewery and restaurant. He's been friends with Rolf for a while. Berkley met them while they were traveling and all of them became friends."

"It's almost been a hundred years," Berkley confirmed.

"Tess is our friend who we met in college. She's a witch and is mated to Sam. Sam is a werewolf. Shaye was human, mated to Rolf, they are both vampires. Emma is Rolf's mam, a vampire, and mated to Doc. Doc is the town's doctor and is a shifter. Gawain is a shifter, friends with Rolf. He met his mate Merri, a witch who is also Tess's sister. Then there's me, vampire, and Berkley, Fae," Ian clarified, forgetting his da' hadn't been in the room when he was telling it to his mam.

"And ye all live in the one house?" James asked incredulously.

Ian nodded.

Berkley spoke up with a grin. "Rolf bought land and had built a small house on it before I met him. It was tight when the three of us were there at the same time. He's always been good with money and eventually bought more land and built the house he has now. I think he always wanted a Clan of his own but had been afraid his father would see it as a power play and cause problems."

"That would explain why he had such a big house." Ian grinned at Berkley before turning back to his parents. "So, Tess and Sam go to visit her family for about a week. On their way home, they were attacked by the remains of Vlad's minions. They were hoping to take over Vlad's empire. Not sure if they thought picking us off would be the way to build a reputation, or what. They had hired a lone witch who cast a death spell on Sam. Luckily Tess had put a protection spell around him, so it stopped it from instantly killing him, but he was trapped in wolf form and the spell was resistant to witch healing. Merri drove them home and Shaye and Doc were able to use her healing magic and everyone else's non-witch magic to save Sam. Emma and Doc finally claimed each other at New Year's. We celebrated Doc's birthday and then they found an orphaned wolf pup. It turned out he was a wolf-dog hybrid and we've all taken turns feeding him and taking him out. He's such a tiny thing right now, it's hard to picture him as a big wolf," Ian finished.

His mam just stared at him.

"What? Did I miss something?" Ian asked Berkley. He thought he hit all the points without getting into too much detail.

Berkley shook his head, trying not to grin. Ian's mom looked shell-shocked after Ian's info dump.

"Mam. Mam, what's the face for?" Ian asked.

Berkley took another scone, sitting back to watch the scene unfold. He noticed James doing the same thing. James passed him the clotted cream with an eye roll. Berkley coughed to cover up his snort of laughter.

"That was all from November to the New Year," she said flatly, not making it into a question.

"Yes," Ian drew out.

"Ye were in danger twice and didnae tell us!"

"Mam, it was only one fight. I didnae even hae a scratch on me. The thing with Sam just kept us busy, I was no' in danger. They killed the attackers, so there's no more threat there. Plus, look." Ian drew out the pendant from underneath his shirt. "Berkley made everyone pendants. They glow if there's danger nearby. Only we can see the alert; to anyone walking by they look normal. Cool, huh?"

"Thank ye for looking after my daft son," Charlotte told Berkley.

"I'm no' daft!" Ian shouted indignantly.

James cleared his throat, his mouth twitching. "Weel, son. That all sounds very interesting. What are ye going to do now that it's going to be boring?"

"I'm leatherworking right now. If the store next door to Berkley's shop goes up for sale, we'll buy it and put in a connecting door. I'll hae a physical store then and the online store. Rolf has offered to build us a workshop at the house. I wanted to see if ye had any ideas on a design while we were here," Ian told his da'.

"That sounds fun," his da' agreed. "There's a couple forges up north as weel, if ye wanted to see different options."

Ian looked at Berkley. "Maybe we can take a day trip?"

"There's a market and craft fair going on in a couple of

days up there too," his mam pointed out. "Ian, ye are to call me if ye are in danger again, do ye understand me?"

"Yes, mam," Ian agreed to keep the peace. It's not like they ever left the farm and there wasn't anything she could do about it from here. He still wasn't sure why she would want to know; as long as he wasn't gravely injured, he would be fine, and she wouldn't have to worry about him for no good reason. But his mam wanted to know, so he supposed he would call if anything happened again.

"I'm going to get dinner started. James why don't ye take them to your forge and let them see it," Charlotte said, standing up and brushing off her skirt.

"Follow me, boys," his father said, grabbing his coat off the rack.

"Ian. Son. Ye ken that your mam worries about ye. I understand why ye didnae tell her all of it before, but for my sake, please tell her when shite happens from now on," his dad said once they were out of the house.

"Sure, Da'," Ian replied.

His da' walked to his forge, unlocking the large wood doors. "I hae no' used it much lately, but you can get an idea."

Berkley looked around as they walked inside. The forge was made of stone, a squarish base, with the chimney going through the ceiling. There was a large hearth for the combustible materials to go, with a stone water trough in front. The anvil sat close by off to the side. The walls were covered with his tools.

"What kind of forge are ye thinking ye want?" James asked as Ian explored.

"I hae some ideas, but I'm no' set on one design yet. Most of the things I'm going to make will be items for general sale, but I would like to be able to make some bespoke pieces for custom orders. My current forge is a small propane one that I used while traveling. All the forges I've been near lately hae been propane as well, since it's been a lot of other travelers. But I wanted to look at yours again. I once saw a really cool wood forge, and we hae the forest nearby with plenty of fallen logs, but that type does require more work. I'm thinking of having a coal-fueled forge, but gas might be easier. An electric fan blower for the air supply would be easiest, if I'm going to be making a lot of pieces. But traditional bellows are so cool looking," Ian said.

"If ye have the room, why no' hae a coal and a propane? That way ye would get the heat ye would need. I think wood would be too much hassle. Most home-sized propane forges are smaller, so ye would be limited on your project size. If ye hae the coal forge, ye would need a chimney and a good air supply, but ye could use it for larger projects or for a more traditional feel. I would go with the electric motor blower. They take up so much less room and make it easier. I switched to a hand-cranked fan blower when I redid the forge. Skip the bellows, trust me."

"That would be cool," Berkley said. "I'd love to see what you could do with both types of forges. If we're still thinking of having the forge and the kiln under one roof, we may need to have a separate room for the ceramics, so any coal smoke doesn't contaminate the pieces."

"That's true," Ian said. "I didnae think of that. It's been a while since I've used one, but as ye can see from Da's, they can leave smoke residue. We may need separate air ducts as well. Da', how long do we hae until dinner?"

"I think your mam was making a roast, so a few hours. Why?"

"Let's fire it up. I saw these really neat flowers someone posted online and wanted to give it a try. Mam would like it, I think," Ian replied.

Ian stepped back as his da' fired up the forge, getting it up to temperature. "Which pieces are okay for me to use?" Ian asked, looking around.

"Anything from over here is good to use. That corner is all spoken for," James replied.

Ian grabbed gloves and an apron and set about making a rose for his mam. His da' stood by and watched as it came together. The heat felt good, his muscles working hard and his brain concentrating on forming the petals. It had been too long since he had been in a forge; he really needed to get the plans finalized so they could build in the spring. This was one of his happy places and he missed how the focus made his mind quiet.

Berkley stood to the side, watching his mate work. Ian now had a fine sheen of sweat. Berkley could only imagine just how those muscles looked under the shirt. Hmm, it was probably a good thing that they would need a dividing wall between their workspaces, or he would never get anything done. He would be imagining Ian working shirtless, the sweat dripping down his abs, rolling down the six-pack to the V at his hips. Yum.

Ian stepped away, holding the still hot flower. It looked amazing. Berkley loved it. James grabbed a pair of tongs and started heating some metal. It seemed like he was going to give it a try as well. In the end, by the time Ian's mom poked her head in to tell them dinner was almost ready, Ian and his dad both had a finished rose to give to her. Berkley thought those would sell extremely well at Valentine's Day and Mother's Day. Ian helped his dad shut down the forge and they stopped to wash at the sink by the door. Berkley loved that they found something in common to bond over, as he watched them discuss techniques they could use to make different types of flowers.

When they got inside the house, Ian's mom was pulling food out of the stove. "Did ye hae fun?"

"Aye. Ian showed me a new trick," James said, smiling.

"Oh? What was it?" she asked.

"Char, ye got to look," James said.

She put the food on top of the stove, removing the oven mitts and setting them on the counter before turning around. "What?"

Ian and his dad pulled the roses out from behind their backs at the same time. "For you, Mam," Ian said, walking over to give her a kiss on the cheek.

"Oh, those are lovely! I'll always hae flowers now. Thank ye, my lads," she said, giving her husband and son a kiss.

Dinner was delicious and Berkley thought the conversation was a lot less awkward than it had been at tea. He helped clear the table and dried the dishes as Ian washed. It was getting late, but Ian asked if his parents wanted to play a game.

"What kind of game?" Charlotte asked.

"I brought one from home. It's easy and quick, but we always hae lots of fun with it. I think our bags are still in the car, so let me go grab them."

Berkley went out with him to grab the rest of their luggage.

"Okay, so it's called Furglars," Ian said as he started setting up the game. "Ye roll the die. Your goal is to get as many furgles as possible, the little green fuzzy side of the dice. If ye get an X, ye get nothing from that dice. If ye get a lock, keep it to protect your furgles from being stolen. A hand is used to steal someone's lock or furgle. If ye hae two hands and they hae a lock and a furgle, ye use one hand to steal the lock and one to steal the furgle. Turn your furgles in for these bars and this tells ye what they're worth," Ian explained, pointing to one of the boards. "Watch out for Berkley. He always manages to get a ton of locks," he warned.

"Hey!" Berkley protested. It was true though. He might not always have a furgle to protect, but he somehow ended up rolling a bunch of locks.

"Sounds easy enough," James said. He grabbed a couple

of glasses and a bottle of whiskey. "Anyone for an after-dinner drink?"

Charlotte declined, making herself a pot of tea, but Ian and Berkley both took a glass.

"Oh! Da', I forgot I had something for ye," Ian said suddenly. He ran over to his suitcase and pulled out a bottle of the Oban that he had bought them. "I took Berkley on a tour and picked this up for ye. Oban's a cute town. It's no' too far away if ye and mam ever wanted to see it."

"They do make a decent whiskey," James replied, grinning at the gift.

The game went fairly quickly, and it encouraged conversation and laughter. Ian's mom won the first game, crushing them with her furgle rolling capabilities. Pretty soon though, both James and Charlotte were yawning, having stayed up later than normal. Ian let his parents get ready for bed first, cleaning up the game and their glasses. As his parents finished in the bathroom, Ian took Berkley outside for a walk.

"I think that went pretty well," Berkley said.

"Much better than I had anticipated," Ian agreed. "But there's something that I hae been wanting to do all night," he told Berkley as he pulled him back by the woodshed.

"What's that?" Berkley asked with a grin. He thought he knew where this was going.

Once they were out of sight from the house, Ian shoved Berkley against the shed wall, grinding their hips together. He grabbed Berkley's face, pulling him in for a kiss.

'I love ye, my Fae,' Ian told him, his tongue exploring Berkley's mouth, twisting against his tongue. 'We hae to be quick,' he added as he reached down and unzipped his pants before moving to unfasten Berkley's as well. He drew his head back from the kiss only to spit in his hand, gripping their cocks together. Berkley pulled his face back for a kiss, his breath coming faster as Ian jerked them off. Letting go for a moment, Ian lined their cocks up, pulling his foreskin over

Berkley's cockhead, docking them together. Leaning forward he took Berkley's mouth in another kiss, their tongues tangling together, as Ian jerked them off. Ian hissed as Berkley tugged on his barbells, sending shocks of pleasure down to his balls. It only took them a couple of minutes before they were coming, panting hard and grinning like idiots at each other.

'Let's clean up and head to bed. I have a feeling your parents are early risers.' Normally Berkley would be self-conscious about what they just did in the outdoors, but there weren't any neighbors in viewing distance and Ian's bed was only a box bed with a curtain, no real doors to keep their noises quiet.

The house was still as they made their way back in. Ian locked the door behind them. Finding their toothbrushes, they made a quick stop in the bathroom before climbing into bed. Berkley took the wall side, Ian moving to pull the curtains closed. They could hear faint snoring from his parents' bed.

'Night, love,' Berkley said.

'*Goodnight, mo chridhe,*' Ian said, rolling over to kiss him gently.

9

"What do ye think of driving up to see the market and the forge tomorrow?" Ian asked.

"That sounds good. What time would we need to leave?"

"Hmm, maybe around eight or nine, nothing too crazy. We can always come home late if we're having a great time or find a room to stay in. I want to stop at an ATM if we can find one. Markets and craft fairs don't always take credit cards, so I want to hae some extra cash on hand. I hae a feeling we're going to find some treasures there," Ian said, grinning.

"I do love treasure hunts," Berkley agreed. His magic was a little restless this morning. He could feel it buzzing, poking at him almost, but when he sent it a questioning glance it gave the equivalent of a shrug. It looked like it didn't know why it was wound up either. Great. "Should we invite your parents? Do you think they would like to come along?" He knew they didn't go out a lot, but they were here to visit with them and didn't want them to feel left out.

"We can ask," Ian replied. He wasn't sure if they would go or not.

His parents declined, saying they didn't have anything

they needed to buy at the moment. Ian thought maybe they needed a break from having visitors.

That next morning, Berkley almost asked if they could stay at home and skip their outing. Ian had dressed himself in a kilt, complete with a sporran, a small dagger in his sock, and a pair of black leather boots. He had paired it with a t-shirt and a tight zip-up sweater. He looked incredibly sexy, and Berkley wanted to find out if he was wearing the kilt the traditional way.

"Nope," Ian said as he caught Berkley watching him. "Ye can find out when we're done wi' our trip." He may have to wear a kilt more when they got back home, he thought when he saw how turned-on Berkley was.

They passed through a decent-sized town that had a bank with an ATM. It took a couple of hours to get to the blacksmith, but the sun was out, and it wasn't freezing. Ian got out of the car and looked around. It was a plain, almost warehouse type of building. Walking into the small reception area they saw a bell at the front desk, but no receptionist. Ringing the bell, they waited while Ian walked around looking at the pictures on the wall. They made some nice pieces here. Not really what he was into, but still nice.

"Hello, can I help ye?" a voice said behind him. Turning around, he saw a man about his age, well his human-looking age.

"Hi. I'm sorry to barge in, but I was wondering if I could talk to the master blacksmith here."

"Uh, that's my da'. Let me go fetch him," the kid responded, leaving them to wait for a couple of minutes.

A man came around the corner. He was solidly built, tall, broad, with plenty of muscles. "Can I help ye? My son said ye wanted to talk to me."

"Hello, my name is Ian. I wanted to see if ye had time to talk about your forge? I'm also a blacksmith, but I live in America now. I'm setting up my own permanent forge and hae been trying to decide on a layout, coal versus propane, that type of thing. My da' has a small forge of his own a couple hours south of here and he recommended stopping in and seeing some other workshops."

"Graeme," he replied, reaching out to shake Ian's hand. "Do ye have a website, or something that can prove ye are a blacksmith? I can no' take customers into the workshop due to insurance and liability reasons, but if ye are a blacksmith then ye ken how to be there safely," he explained.

"I do," Ian replied, pulling out his phone and showing his website. "This is me. I do leatherwork and blacksmithing. It was a travel job for a while, but I'm settling down and looking to create my own space."

Graeme took the phone, scrolling through. "These are great. We dinnae make quite the same things," he looked up with a smile.

"I was working festivals for a bit, so my latest work tends to be the things that would sell there. Although I did make a rose at my da's recently. I'm thinking of adding those to the shop once I have it going."

"Ye could try a powder coating on the rose to give it different colors," Graeme suggested.

"That's a good idea. I'll hae to experiment once I get set up."

"Let me grab ye both some gloves and an apron before we head in," he replied, walking into another room.

"I think the powder coating is a great idea," Ian told Berkley. "We could have them in lots of different colors, make a rainbow bouquet. I should play with different types of flowers too, since Emma is more of a wildflower type of lady."

"Here ye go," Graeme said, coming back in, handing them safety glasses, aprons, and gloves. "Just to be safe, there's a couple of the forges running right now."

"How many do ye have?" Ian asked.

"There are six total, three coal and three propane. The coal is great for working on the large pieces. We hae blowtorches for working on smaller areas."

Walking in, Ian took a breath. Even with three coal forges, it wasn't as dusty or smokey as he thought it would be. "Ye hae a great ventilation system in here."

"Thanks. I'll show ye how we hae it set up," Graeme said, walking over to one of the forges not in use.

Berkley followed, but he wasn't listening too much to their conversation. He didn't know much about the process, and he was more interested in watching how excited and happy Ian was. He was animated and almost bouncing on his toes in excitement. They really needed to get their workshop built. He wanted Ian to be this happy every day.

Graeme walked them through the workshop, pointing out things for both types of forges. There was a large window that took up half of a wall and looked to the outside. Berkley wondered if they could install a similar idea between the two sides of their workshop. It would be nice to be able to see his partner while they were both working. They stayed about two hours, with Ian taking notes on his phone. He thanked Graeme before they left.

"That was fun, thank ye for humoring me for so long," Ian said as they got back in the car.

"I'm glad you had fun. Did you get any ideas?" Berkley asked.

"I did. I'll have to sketch it out for ye later. I hae a bunch of notes and pictures that should help too. It was nice to talk to him. Are ye ready to go?" Ian asked as he pulled out of the driveway.

Berkley nodded. "I can't wait to see it. It should be fun. Anything in particular you're looking for?"

"No' really. It would be nice to find some trinkets to bring home, but nothing that I'm really wanting to buy. Ye?"

"Same, nothing really. We'd have to either ship it home or

it would have to fit in the luggage, so unless it's amazing, I'm fine with just browsing and enjoying seeing new things."

It didn't take long to get to the fair, especially since Ian was driving and he tended to have a heavy foot.

Ian pulled into the parking lot, which turned out to be a field they were using for parking. It was already a little crowded, but it was a nice day. The sun was still shining, and it was on the warm side of cool, feeling more like an early spring day. Of course, people were going to come out to enjoy the weather. Hopefully it meant that there were more vendors as well. They ended up parking rather far away, but they were built for walking. He grabbed a reusable bag that his mam had given him. It was nice with long handles, a zippered top, and a plastic-lined interior. He could fit quite a bit in here if they found something they wanted.

"Ready to find some treasures?" Ian asked.

Berkley nodded. He was looking forward to what they might be able to discover. He thought the day was already a win because Ian had such a good time at the blacksmith. Berkley had already started designing his side of the workshop in his head. He needed to sketch it out so Ian could add his design and they could make any needed adjustments. He hoped Rolf wouldn't mind the size of the building. They could always move it farther back from the house. It probably made more sense to have it farther away due to the potential smoke from the forge and fire hazard. They may need to clear some of the trees around the building site as well. He would need to look into any local regulations and safety codes.

Ian started walking to a food booth, looking at the shortbread and meat pies they had available. "Are ye hungry?" he asked.

"Not right now, but you go ahead and get something to eat," Berkley said. He was still full from breakfast.

Ian bought a couple of handheld pies and a bag of cookies for later. He grabbed a bottle of water as well; he had packed a couple in the SUV but had forgotten to grab them when they walked in. Ian ate one of the pies as they walked down the aisle browsing. Stopping at a produce booth, Ian grabbed some nice-looking onions for his mam. He figured they lasted a while and wouldn't go bad in the car. The spinach and lettuces looked tasty, but he was afraid they would wilt by the time they got back to his parents'. There was some lovely jewelry at a booth that he thought the girls might like. He grabbed Emma a tea sampler and Shaye a really neat metal bookmark. It had been embossed in the shape of a dragon over a hoard of books. He thought she would get a kick out of it.

"I bet these types of markets get busy once it's warmer," Ian said. "If we come back wi' the family, we'll hae to stop at some of these. I bet the girls would love it."

"Sam too. He's always looking for new food ideas or spices for the restaurant," Berkley added.

"Gawain would be all over the old books," Ian added, seeing a stack of antique-looking books on a table. "If we came back during the summer, we could see Loch Ness and catch some of the Highland Games. Tess and Shaye would love to see all the kilts," Ian said with a smile.

"Me too," Berkley replied with a smirk, running a quick teasing hand over Ian's ass.

"I'll wear one for ye whenever ye want," Ian promised, his fingers brushing against Berkley's. He'd gotten out of practice wearing his since he'd been in the States. He forgot how much he enjoyed them. Maybe he'd start wearing his more often.

"Hm, I can't wait," Berkley replied, eyeing his partner.

As they strolled down the booths, Berkley saw one that looked interesting and pulled Ian over. The booth had a small cloth-covered table in the front right corner that held crystals and other mystical types of items. There were some display trays of crystals, sage bundles, and there was also a small carousel of postcards. The walls of the booth had a few small photographs and suncatchers hanging along the edge. Compared to the other booths in the aisle, this one was very small in size and only had a limited selection of items for sale. Almost like it had been set up in a hurry, although it was still neat and tidy. It was strange, Berkley thought to himself, but maybe she just wanted something that would be quick to set up and breakdown. *'I think some of these would be good for Tess and Merri,'* he said quietly.

'Is the lady a witch or just selling what she thinks are good tourist trinkets?' Ian asked. It made a difference in how they proceeded with pricing and any conversation they might have with her. He could normally tell another paranormal, but he wasn't sure on this one, which was odd. The booth was a strange mixture of things that seemed genuine, but some of the items even Ian could tell were just for tourists.

'I don't really know. Some of her stuff is authentic, but I think she must be wearing a concealment spell. She's registering as muddled to my senses, even her aura is muted. That doesn't happen naturally, so she must be hiding what she is,' Berkley responded. *'I would guess witch, but I'm not sure why she would need to hide that.'*

Ian took a moment to look at Berkley's pendant. *'It's not glowing, so at the moment it's not registering danger. Would it still pick up on it if she was concealed?'*

'Yes. I'll just assume she's paranormal if we buy anything,' Berkley responded.

'I'll let you take the lead,' Ian replied. He had no real knowledge of the witch and magic side of paranormals, other than what he had seen from Tess and Berkley. He wouldn't know which crystals were real and which were man-made imitations, or how much they should sell for.

"Good afternoon," Berkley greeted the woman. She appeared to be in her late thirties, maybe early forties. Of course, if she was paranormal that number could be way off. "How much are you asking for the crystals?" he asked.

"I believe the ones ye would be interested in are over here," the woman pointed out. "Those are just pretty decorations," she added, pointing to the ones in the front row.

"Thank you," Berkley replied, moving to look at the ones she recommended.

She was definitely a paranormal then, Ian thought as he browsed through the rest of the booth, finding some fun postcards and other odds and ends that were more souvenir than usable in magic.

The woman spoke quietly next to his ear, giving him a start. He should have been able to hear her walking toward him. His pendant was still dull, so he was going to trust in his mate's magic.

"There are some papers here that I believe ye would be interested in," she said, almost in a whisper. Her eyes kept glancing around, making sure no one was paying any attention to what she was pointing out.

"Can I ask what is making ye nervous?" Ian asked just as quietly.

Berkley came to stand near them. It looked like the woman was worried and if she was a paranormal, it might be something they didn't want everyone walking by to overhear. To be on the safe side, he acted like he needed to place his handful of items down and bent over, placing them on the chair behind the table. The chair was short enough that the tablecloth on the table hid his hands from view as he cast a quick spell to mute their conversation and to give them some protection. Standing back up, he made sure to face out of the booth to keep an eye on everyone and to appear like he was still shopping. Scrolling through the postcard stand, he was close enough to hear their conversation, but was in a spot where he would be blocking most people's view of the inside of the booth.

"We've had a bunch of hunters in town the past month. I'm a witch and a Seer, although I'm using a concealment spell, which I'm sure ye noticed. We've no' had any troubles wi' hunters for so long that they caught me by surprise. They've been loitering near any shops or booths that seem in any way magical. I don't know how but they are able to pick out anyone paranormal. I hae warned anyone that comes by my shop; I've been hearing about attacks on paranormals and even rumors that some hae gone missing. I'm leaving today to head to my family's homestead. The magic there is strong and will keep them away," she said as she held up a small stained-glass Celtic knot as if she were trying to convince Ian to buy it. "I hae some documents that I dinnae feel safe keeping wi' me any longer and my visions told me to come here today. We were meant to meet, and I ken these papers belong wi' your Clan. Keep them safe and don't let the hunters get them," she warned. She pulled out a packet of old papers and some ancient-looking thin manuscripts that were encased in a waterproof bag from her handbag. She handed them to Ian, standing at an angle to help conceal Ian stuffing the package under his shirt. He unzipped his sweater so that it would hang open, hoping the looseness of it would help hide the fact that he had placed the documents in the small of his back. When he was finished, she moved around the booth, pointing out a few other stained-glass pieces, a High-land cattle photograph, and finally a woolen scarf. As she stepped back to her chair, gathering up the items Berkley had laid out, she gave Berkley a tiny nod to release the sound spell.

"Is this all for ye, then?" she asked, beginning to ring up the items on her phone.

"How much are the postcards?" Berkley asked, making small talk like they would with any booth.

"Three for a pound for the larger ones, four for a pound for the small ones," she replied.

Berkley glanced over his shoulder at Ian. "What do you think about these?" he asked, showing Ian several postcards.

"I love those," he replied. "Can we get the stained-glass piece ye were showing me, as weel? I think that would look grand in the kitchen window," he added. He didn't want to draw any attention to the woman and buying the piece she had been showing him earlier might help with that.

"Aye, it's a lovely piece," she said with a smile. "It will bring happiness to those in your home." Ian wondered if that meant it was spelled. He would ask Berkley later. He had been hoping to spend the night here, but if hunters were nearby, he wanted to get back to the safety of his parents' farm. There were spells on the land to protect it. He should have gotten Emma's address as well to act as a backup. He knew she had protections on it from those who wished to do harm.

'Emma?' he asked tentatively. He hadn't used the Clan link very much, plus he wasn't sure if she would be awake.

'Ian? Is everything alright?' she asked, concerned.

'It is at the moment. We're at a market and a woman just warned us of hunters in the area. I ken we're a bit far away, but I was wondering if I could get the address of your farm, just in case we need another safe spot,' he asked.

'Of course, you can go there if you need to! I'll let Samantha know and send her and Douglas pictures of you just in case you need to go. Douglas gets protective of strangers near the property, even with the protection spells. Be safe,' she added before giving him the address and quick directions to her property.

'Thank ye, Emma. I feel better knowing we hae another place to go. I do no' like how we are hearing about hunters at home and here. I was hoping they had all died out,' he replied.

'Keep us updated,' Emma said.

Ian tuned back into the conversation between Berkley and the woman as they finished the sale transaction.

"Will ye be okay leaving?" Ian asked quietly, concerned.

"Aye. This will only take me a minute to pack up. I'm only taking the real items with me, and they all fit in my handbag. I'm leaving the rest so it looks like I just went to the restroom," she replied. She handed Ian a small satchel hidden under the bubble-wrapped glass.

"Keep this on ye, opposite side of your bracelet," she said, sliding it into his hand. "They're coming and this will help ye. Keep faith in your mate's magic and in your family," she murmured mysteriously as they started to walk out of her booth.

'I asked Emma if it was alright to use her farm as another safe location,' Ian told Berkley. He passed on the address and the directions Emma had given him. *'Having hunters around is making me nervous,'* he added.

'Do you want to leave now?' Berkley asked, pausing to look at a soap booth.

'No. We should wait a few minutes to make sure she can leave and it doesn't look suspicious. I dinnae want to draw attention to her,' Ian added. They could walk the rest of the aisle and then head back to their car. It would at least appear that they had finished shopping and were heading out, not that she had said something to cause them to leave as soon as they met with her.

'Do you know what she gave you?' Berkley asked.

'No, she just said it was important papers that should be with our Clan. I never mentioned us having a Clan, but she said she was a Seer, so maybe that's how she knew. She did say she had a vision about us,' Ian replied. *'I'll hae a look when we get back to Mam's. I dinnae feel safe looking at it out here if there are hunters nearby. Nothing this old should be in their hands.'*

Berkley bought a couple bars of the heather soap and added it to their shopping bag. They stopped to watch a demonstration at a candle-making booth, before walking on. Ian bought a new sporran and a lovely deep blue cable knit wool sweater for Berkley. He thought the color would make

Berkley's eyes pop. They reached the end of the aisle when he noticed Berkley's necklace began to glow. He took a peek down his own shirt to find his glowing as well.

'*Ber,*' Ian warned.

'*I see it. I can't sense where they are,*' he replied, frustrated. '*Can you give me a hug? I want to cast an invisibility type of spell on those documents and don't want to be obvious about it.*'

'*I'll always give ye a hug, love,*' Ian replied. Moving forward, he loosely wrapped his arms around his mate and laid his head on his shoulder. He was looking back at the crowd, trying to see if anyone was focused on them. He left it loose enough that Berkley had room to make the spell. Ian's sweater flared around them, hiding Berkley's hands even more. Luckily it was daylight, so it would be harder to see if this spell caused a light to flare. Ian wasn't sure why some spells had a light flash and others didn't; he should really ask Berkley to explain the difference to him one day. '*I don't see anyone in the crowd staring at us, but there are a few guys on the hill looking this way.*' Ian squinted, trying to see them a little better. The sunlight glinted off something on their persons, but he couldn't tell if it was a weapon or not.

'*Let's head to the car,*' Berkley said. '*Maybe we can get away before they catch up to us. Walk like we haven't noticed them, but a little faster than before,*' he added. He took the shopping bag and threaded his arms through the handles to wear it like a backpack. It would leave his arms and hands free. '*Did you bring any weapons today?*' he asked.

'*I have the sgain-dubh in my sock,*' Ian replied. The small knife wouldn't give too much protection in a fight, as the short blade meant that he would need to be closer to their enemies to use it, but he supposed that it was better than nothing. He could only hope they would make it safely to the car and get out of here before the men caught up to them.

Berkley nodded. "Are you getting hungry?" he asked aloud, for anyone listening nearby.

"I could eat. Do ye want to see what they hae for dinner?" Ian asked, holding on to Berkley's hand as they walked to the car. Normally they were pretty careful not to hold hands in a rural environment in case the people there were closed-minded, but he wanted to be able to grab Berkley and run if he needed to. He could carry his mate and still run extremely fast. If he could get them away from the crowd, it would give them more opportunity to use their paranormal gifts in a fight.

They started walking toward the parking lot, listening intently for the sounds of anyone following them. Ian noticed that the woman who had given them the documents wasn't in her booth, so hopefully she had safely left before the hunters arrived. Their pendants still glowed, alerting them that the danger remained close. Reaching the field, Ian noticed a few men standing in the lot. He let go of Berkley's hand to wrap his arm around his waist, knowing he could grab him like a football if he needed to run.

"Should we pick something up on the way home, or do you want to eat out?" Berkley asked. He pulled up the camera on his phone, acting like he was going to scroll for food places nearby. Instead, he opened the camera and changed it to selfie mode, using it to look behind him. He took a few shots of the men following them. He sent them off to Rolf with a message that there may be trouble. He didn't know if they had any identifying marks on them to show which hunter group they belonged to. He snapped a few more pictures, zooming in on the men's faces. They had something pinned on their shirts, but he couldn't make it out. He figured Gage might be able to find out and quickly sent him a text message with the situation details.

They were halfway to the car when they heard a shout behind them. "Hey, ye two! I ken what ye are, demons."

Ignoring the man, they kept walking, talking about nothing in particular trying to seem normal.

'Demon? Really? Do they think all paranormals are demons, or are these just religious nuts?' Ian asked.

A man appeared in front of them, a gun discreetly tucked into his waistband, the jacket almost covering it. Berkley snapped another picture, sending it. This time he could clearly see the symbol on the man's clothes, although he wasn't familiar with it.

"I believe my brother was talking to ye," he said gruffly.

"I'm sorry, do I know ye?" Ian asked, his muscles tensing in preparation.

"Nae. But we ken what ye are," the man boasted.

"What we are? Gay?" Ian asked, pretending like he was confused. "Weel, we were holding hands, so I think that was pretty obvious."

"Dinnae be dense. We ken ye are demons," the man claimed.

"I hate to tell you, but we're not demons," Berkley said. He whispered a few words under his breath. Once he felt a new weight around his neck, he reached into his shirt to pull out the new cross necklace. "See? We're just here on vacation. Please let us pass."

"That proves nothing," the man said, but he didn't sound as confident as before. "See, our da' gave us this demon finder. It lights up when there's demons nearby," he said, showing them a cross with a spelled glass center that was currently glowing.

There were footsteps behind them, and they were suddenly wet.

"What the hell was that?" Berkley shouted at them.

"Holy water," the other man said smugly.

"What was the point of that?" Ian asked. He didn't like that these men were still fixated on them. He was very happy that the documents were in a waterproof bag.

"To weaken ye or kill ye."

"Listen, we're out in broad daylight, the holy water isn't

harming us, and we hae a cross necklace that we're wearing. I don't ken what your da' is playing at, but we're no' demons," Ian replied. "Leave us alone."

'Berkley? It's Rolf. Gage said another Warden can reach you guys and help; it's the same one who collected the bodies after the attack on Sam and Tess. His name is Marco and he's on his way to you. Gage said that Marco needs to stop here first to get something of yours so that he can track you. He teleports but has a hard time pinpointing exact locations without something to guide him.'

'We could use the help,' Berkley responded. *'These guys are armed and have a necklace that glows near paranormals. Although they think we're demons, so they're not the most knowledgeable of hunters. They already threw holy water on us. Of course, other than being cold now, it didn't do anything but that's not stopping them,'* Berkley replied.

'I'll tell Gage to have Marco hurry up. Use magic if you need to. Stay safe, we're here although I'm not sure how we can help from so far away,' Rolf admitted, frustration in his voice.

"Maybe he's right," the man who threw the water at them said. "Nothing's happening. The holy water should have worked by now."

"That witch gave them something, I know it. Hand it over," the man said stubbornly.

"We bought some postcards, a stained-glass Celtic knot and some pretty rocks for our windowsill. That was it. You probably ruined our postcards with the water stunt, so thanks for that." Berkley pulled Ian with him as he started moving for their car. If he could get them inside, he could throw a spell around it, keeping them safe.

"Eh! I'm no' done with ye yet," the man protested. "I got questions."

"Listen, leave us alone and we won't call the police," Berkley said. "I'm sure they would love to hear that someone is harassing tourists."

"Bert, let's go," water guy said. "Sean and I are leaving. This was a mistake."

"Bert, how are ye going to live up to your da's reputation if ye don't stand your ground? Do ye always want to live in his shadow? Or do ye want to make a name for yourself?" a new voice said, goading the man in front of them. Ian looked behind him, seeing the group from the hill had caught up to them.

Great, new bullies, Ian thought. They were definitely now outnumbered, and Ian was starting to get really worried.

'Rolf said help is on the way, but I don't know how close he is,' Berkley said. *'Should we try to run to the car? Or if we make a big scene, they might back off if we get more people around,'* he suggested.

Ian looked around the parking lot. *'I don't think there's enough people for that to work. I think for them to back off we would need them to be outnumbered, and right now there aren't that many other people around. Plus, if stupid gets a shot off, a human could be killed.'* The peer pressure might get these men to back down, but he also didn't want to take the chance that an innocent bystander could get hurt as well. He and Berkley had a better chance of surviving an injury than a human would.

"Trust the detector," the new guy encouraged. "Take them out now. Ye will be doing the world a service. Even if the necklace is wrong, it will send a message we dinnae want their kind here."

Ian snorted. A homophobic hunter. Lovely. It had been such a great date day too. He grabbed Berkley tighter.

'I'm going to run, hold tight. I'll try to get us to the passenger side of the SUV so it's between us and them. At this point, I don't care if they see the paranormal stuff. I think they're unhinged.'

"Bert, if they're just tourists, that's murder. I don't care if they're holding hands, ye can't kill them for that," the water thrower protested. "I'm out of here. Ye are crazy. I never should hae listened to ye." The man ripped the pin off his coat and left, another man following after him.

Well, that was two less, but they still had a group of five. It would have been nice if the man had called the police on his buddies or helped them in some way, Berkley thought. *'I'm ready,'* Berkley replied, grabbing onto Ian's waist.

The man pulled out his gun, pointing it at them. Ian's heart sped up in fear when he saw the resignation and deter-mination on the man's face. They had never learned the answer on if Doc's immortality meant they could still be killed or not. The Fae's immortality simply meant that they lived forever; however, although it was extremely hard, there were still some ways to kill them. He couldn't let his mate get shot, he thought as he watched the man pull the trigger in slow-motion. Ian used his speed to push Berkley out of the way. He was hoping that he would be fast enough to get out of the way as well, but he felt a searing pain in his chest as his body fell. Dual lights flashed as the bullet hit his body, from his wrist and from his pocket where the witch's satchel was.

"That was coated in holy water, blessed by a priest, and rubbed with salt. Guaranteed to kill a demon," the man said smugly.

"A bullet will kill anyone, you idiot," Berkley shouted, grabbing for Ian.

Ian watched as Berkley dropped to his knees next to him, covering his body with his own. *'Run, love,'* Ian told his mate, looking in horror behind him as the man cocked the gun again. Berkley ignored his words, shaking his head as his hands moved to form a spell. There was a rushing roar of wind as he lay there, feeling the blood seep from his body into the dirt. The men who had surrounded them now lay on the ground, handcuffed and feet bound together.

"I'm Marco. I'm so sorry I couldn't get here sooner," the new man said. "I'll deal with this bunch if you want to take him to your car and get him healed up." This must be the Warden that Gage was sending.

Ian could feel himself getting weaker, he knew the bullet was still in his body, although how it didn't go through him was a mystery. The man shot him at close range.

'Ian Freckles Douglas! I am going to kick your ass when you get home!' a scared voice shouted in his head.

Ian felt the Clan link open and suddenly everyone was crowding in his head. Shaye had opened the link on her end.

'Berkley, I've got the bullet stabilized. It's in his heart, so move him carefully to the back seat of your car,' she instructed, her voice thick with tears. *'Ian, you hang on. I'm not about to lose my brother now.'*

Berkley looked at Marco. "Can you grab my keys and open the door for me?"

The other man nodded. Making a gesture with his hand, their attackers now lay there unconscious. "I'll block this area from the humans and deal with these guys later. They're going to a Warden facility. You won't have to worry about them again," he said as he took the keys. With one more gesture, the men disappeared. He helped Berkley lift Ian and once Berkley had a good hold on him, Marco followed them to their car and opened the back seat. "I put a protection on your car. The humans won't see what's going on. That protection bag she gave you and your bracelet really helped," he added. "The bullet would have torn through his heart otherwise. That immortality is doing its job too; but just the same, you shouldn't leave the bullet in there as it will keep him weak even if it won't kill him." Marco gave him a nod before disappearing.

Berkley couldn't let himself dwell on that right now. He laid Ian down, not liking how pale he was.

'What should I do?' he frantically asked their family. His mate was in pain and had a bullet stuck in his heart.

'Place your hands over the wound,' Shaye told him. *'I could

feel when he got shot and I never want you guys to do that again. Do you understand?' she demanded, sounding scared. *'I'm going to keep his heart intact, but you're going to have to get the bullet out. Try using magic first, I'd rather you not do surgery in the back seat and a regular hospital won't understand how he's not dead already.'*

Ian's eyes were open, watching him. *'Love ye, Berkley. You're going to hae to hold me down, I think.'* His body's natural reaction would be to move away from the pain and any movement when trying to remove a bullet would be bad.

Berkley's eyes filled with tears. He nodded, using his magic to bind his mate in place. He ripped the bullet hole in the t-shirt larger, giving him some room to work. Holding his hand over the wound, he followed Shaye's directions to where the bullet lay. She projected an image in his mind, showing the path the bullet had made through Ian's body. The witch's magic as well as his protective charm on the bracelet had stopped it from going all the way through his heart, but it had lodged in at least a few centimeters with no part of the bullet sticking out for him to grab. Using a removal spell, he used his magic to slowly coax it out using Shaye's link to help see where it should go. Ian gave a scream of pain as the bullet started to move and Berkley paused, hating that he was causing his mate more suffering.

'You have to keep going,' Shaye said, tears in her voice. *'Just a little more Berkley and it will be out of his heart. Once it's clear of the heart, he's going to bleed a lot more internally, so I need to work fast. You need to stay focused on getting it completely out of his body. Doc is going to take over guiding you at that point while I fix his heart. We love you both, you got this,'* she said encouragingly.

Berkley swallowed hard. *'I love you,'* he told Ian. Gritting his teeth, he started pulling the bullet out again. Ian's body broke out in a cold sweat, his eyes rolling back in his head as he passed out. At least he wouldn't feel the rest of it, Berkley thought, relieved. Watching Ian's chest rise and fall, he slowly worked on removing the bullet. He could tell when it left his beloved's heart, a gush of blood pouring from his body. They weren't getting the deposit back on this rental, he thought, borderline hysterically. There was a moment where the picture in his head paused, Doc taking over to guide his hand.

'Almost there, Berkley. You're doing great,' Doc encouraged. 'Shaye's working hard on his heart. He's going to be fine,' he promised.

Berkley could feel the tremor in his hand, sweat dripping down his face. The concentration was taking everything he had, and he was grateful Marco had placed a protection over the car. There was no way he could do this and pay attention to anyone walking by that might see. The bullet popped out of Ian's chest, causing more blood to flow from his body.

'Okay Berkley. Almost there. Put pressure on that wound to slow the bleeding. Shaye is still working on his heart,' Doc told him.

Pressing down, he was thankful Ian wasn't awake for this. He watched through Doc's view as Shaye used her healing gift to repair the damage left behind by the bullet. It took several minutes, but Ian's heart was completely healed, not even a scar. 'Berkley, I'm almost out,' Shaye admitted, exhaustion in her voice. 'Even with everyone here helping, I don't think I'm going to be able to get him to one hundred percent healed. His heart is perfect, which is the big thing. I'm going to do my best on the rest, but there's some muscle repair needed, and it nicked a bone too. I'm working on those now, but the wound may not be completely closed before I'm done. Seal it the best you can, and I'll try again when I get more energy.'

'You can take mine,' he offered.

'No. You need it to help protect both of you and make sure the wards are strong enough at his parents'. You used energy getting the bullet out, you need to save what you have left in case you need it again,' Shaye told him, her words starting to slur together.

He could see the bone pieces fusing and the muscles knitting together. Suddenly, there was a blank spot in the Clan link. *'Shaye?'* he asked worriedly.

'She's alright,' Doc replied. *'She passed out. I think it's the strain of the distance. Even with all of us sharing energy, it's a long way for her to reach out and heal. She did good though, the heart, muscles, and the rib bone are all repaired. Pack what's left of the wound, wrap it tightly. It will start to heal from his own natural paranormal healing, and we'll do another session once she wakes up and feeds. You need to make sure to eat as well to replenish your energy. Ian will need to drink when he wakes up. Do not give him too much of yours to the point where you are weak. From what I know, his parents do not have any magical abilities, so you're the only one there who can cast protections. See if his parents will let him drink from them. If nothing else, even the farm animals will help, although not as much as human blood will. Gage said the protection that Marco put on the car will allow you to speed and not get caught but be careful. We don't need both of you injured,'* Doc told him.

'I will,' Berkley responded. He found a small first aid kit in the car and packed Ian's wound with the gauze and placed a large bandage over it. He sat Ian up, sliding the sweater down his arms. At least it had already been unzipped. Using the roll of elastic bandage, he wrapped it snugly around his chest to hold everything in place. He didn't bother taking Ian's shirt off, he didn't want to move him too much and he was worried about doing any more damage by lifting up his arms. The adhesive bandage should stay well enough on its own, but the elastic bandage would help apply pressure and to keep it all where it belonged. He laid his mate back on the seat, trying to get him as comfortable as possible. His legs kind of hung off the seat at an odd angle, but it was the best he could do right now. He laid Ian's sweater over his legs and his own coat over Ian's chest, hoping it would both keep him warm and that his scent would comfort him. Taking the bag

off his back, he grabbed the cookies before climbing into the driver's seat. His hands shook as he realized they were covered in blood. Grabbing some of the napkins they had thrown in there earlier, he scrubbed it off the best he could. Taking a deep breath to steady himself, he put his seat belt on and put the car in drive.

He sped the whole way home, eating the cookies and trail mix they had left in the car. He heaved a sigh of relief when he reached Ian's parents' driveway. Pulling in, he used his magic to look at the protections around the property and added his own, reinforcing what was already there. Nothing would be getting to his mate, he vowed. The adrenaline that had been keeping him going faded, his head collapsing atop the steering wheel. He gave the horn a honk, knowing he didn't have the strength to lift Ian right now. His door opened.

"Berkley? What's wrong?" James asked, looking around for Ian.

"Ian's been shot. Can you help carry him inside? I don't think I can," Berkley confessed.

James stepped back, holding out a hand for Berkley when he stumbled. "Go sit. Tell Charlotte to get the bed ready. I've got Ian," James instructed.

Berkley stumbled into the house.

"Berkley! What happened?" Charlotte asked.

"Someone shot Ian at the market. James is bringing him in. Shaye healed him as best she could before she passed out from the strain of doing it from so far away. She's going to finish later, but at least the main parts are healed. Ian's still unconscious though. I added some wards to your property to make sure we're all safe. There was a group of hunters at the market, and they caught us right as we were leaving."

Charlotte looked at him closely. "Sit. I'll get some food going in a minute. Let me get the bed ready first." She placed a tea and sugar in front of Berkley. "Drink this first, the sugar will help." She ran to the armoire and pulled out different sheets. Stripping the bed, she laid plastic sheeting down first, then added clean sheets. She grabbed a new blanket as well. James came through the open door, carrying Ian. When Charlotte saw how bloody Ian was, she swayed a bit before pulling herself together. Grabbing another plastic sheet, she laid it down on top of the cotton sheets she had just put on the bed. James laid Ian gently down.

Berkley came over to help take Ian's clothes off. Unbuckling his kilt, he learned that his man had gone the traditional route. He hadn't noticed in the rush to get him in the car and home. As he pulled the material from underneath Ian, the packet of papers fell to the floor. He had completely forgotten about them in the chaos. He placed them in his suitcase, setting a quick protection and anti-theft spell over his bag. He wasn't worried about Ian's parents, more of when they flew back home. Charlotte grabbed a pair of scissors to finish cutting off Ian's shirt, even cutting through the arm holes so they wouldn't have to lift his arms. James lifted Ian's shoulders off the bed, allowing Berkley to slide the shirt out. Charlotte grabbed a wet washcloth to clean up the dried blood sticking to Ian's chest. She got as much off as she could around the bandages, patting him dry with another towel so they could lay him back on the bed.

"Do you have any first aid supplies?" Berkley asked. He had used most of the useful ones in the car.

"No, but James can run into town to get some," Charlotte said, looking at her husband. "What all do you need?"

"Some gauze pads, or a roll of gauze if they don't have the individual pads. Maybe medical tape, antibiotic cream, and more elastic bandages? I'm hoping Shaye recovers quickly and can finish healing him, but if she's too worn out at least we'll have what we need," Berkley replied.

James nodded, grabbing his keys and heading out the door. "I'm just going to our town, so I'll be quick."

"Hold on!" Berkley shouted. He looked at James, seeing only a watch in terms of jewelry. "May I?" he asked, pointing to the watch.

James undid the clasp, handing it over, looking confused.

Berkley held it in his hands, spelling it to not break or lose time. He finished it with the same protection spell their pendants had. He handed it back to James. "Here, this shouldn't die or break now. I think Marco, the Warden who helped us, got all the hunters that were there, and I didn't see anyone follow us home, but your watch is now spelled to glow if danger is nearby. I put more protection spells on the property, so it should be safe while you are here. When you're out in town or anywhere else, the watch will at least give you a warning. I can make you one tomorrow," he told Charlotte. "I'm out of juice for today," he tried to joke, his body feeling weak, his knees barely holding him up.

James awkwardly patted Berkley on the back before placing the watch on his wrist and leaving.

"Thank ye, Berkley. Now sit. Ye need to eat and so will Ian when he wakes up. Ian will need to drink as well?" she asked as she started pulling out ingredients.

Berkley nodded and collapsed in a kitchen chair. "I can feed him for a little bit, but he will probably need more than what I can give him. He lost a lot."

Charlotte placed a plate full of cheese, crackers, and sliced meat in front of him. "Eat. James and I can feed him. We have a couple of large cows that we drink from, if it comes to that. I imagine they could give quite a bit. We'll rotate feedings and make sure all of us drink lots of water. I'll make a rare beef tonight, that should help as well."

Berkley cleaned the plate off quickly. He hadn't realized he was so hungry.

"Go rest," Charlotte urged. "Ye can sleep on the couch or try our bed," she offered.

"Thank you, I think I'll just sit near Ian." He needed to be close to his partner, to see his chest rise and fall, to hear his poor heart beating.

Berkley took one of the kitchen chairs and set it near the end of the bed so he could look at Ian's face. He sat, his right arm resting on the bed, reaching up to grab Ian's hand. *'You're safe now. Rest and heal. I love you,'* he told Ian. Listening to his rhythmic breathing, Berkley's eyes started to close, the pause between blinks getting longer until he finally fell asleep, slumping forward on the edge of the bed.

A light shake on his shoulder woke Berkley. He opened his eyes to see he had been covered in a blanket. Ian was still asleep.

"Dinner's ready soon," Charlotte told him. "I thought ye should probably eat and then ye can sleep in bed with Ian. You're going to get a sore neck sleeping in the chair."

"I don't want to jostle him," Berkley explained.

"He's still unconscious," Charlotte pointed out. "Plus, I think he would feel better knowing ye are close. James is back with the supplies. He said nothing was out of place in town. It's rare we get visitors, so it's always the big gossip if anyone comes through. Nothing was being talked about, so he doesn't think any hunters visited in town. Why don't ye wash up for dinner? I'm going to call James in from the barn in a few minutes," Charlotte said.

Berkley looked down at himself. His clothes were covered in Ian's blood, and he still had some stuck to his hands and arms from holding him. "I'll grab a quick shower, if there's time?" he asked.

Charlotte nodded, patting him gently on the back. "There's a fresh towel and washcloth in there. Dinner has about twenty minutes left."

Berkley walked to the bathroom, grabbing his pajamas on

the way. It was late and he just wanted to be comfortable. He dropped his clothes in a pile. They were probably trash at this point, he thought. Luckily, he had packed another pair of jeans and a sweatshirt in his suitcase. He'd buy a new coat if they saw one on the way home. He stood under the hot water, breath catching as he saw the rusty colored water running down the drain. He could have lost his mate today. If they hadn't mated, if they hadn't joined the Clan or Doc's tribe, Ian wouldn't have had immortality and that bullet would have killed him. Berkley rested his head on the tiles, biting his fist as he sobbed, all the anxiety and concern and fear finally coming out. He sank to the floor, quietly crying for his Ian.

'Berkley, it will be alright. I promise. Ian will be fine. We're here for you,' he heard Rolf tell him quietly. He felt the warmth of a hug, even though Rolf was thousands of miles away. He felt Emma's light touch, Doc's pat on his shoulder. His family was still with him, he wasn't alone.

'Thank you,' he said, drawing in a deep breath. He stood up and grabbed the soap. If he was going to be sleeping in the same bed as Ian, he didn't want to bring dirt or germs near the still healing wound. He scrubbed until his skin turned pink and he couldn't find any traces of blood left on him. Getting out, he gave his hair a quick brush and threw it into a braid. The soft pajama bottoms and loose t-shirt helped settle him down a little more, as did the filling meal Charlotte had put together. There was plenty of meat and fresh vegetables, along with freshly baked bread for instant carbs. Everyone had large glasses of water at their seats.

"Charlotte, I was wondering if you could help me change the bandages?" Berkley asked as he helped clean up the table.

"Of course," she said. Together they managed to get the old gauze off. She grabbed another washcloth to wipe Ian down again, getting a few spots they had missed earlier. The bullet hole was a little smaller, Berkley thought. He applied some antibiotic cream to the gauze pad and taped it down.

Berkley held Ian sitting up while Charlotte wrapped the elastic bandage around his chest to help ensure it would stay in place if Ian moved around in his sleep. She pulled the plastic sheet out from under Ian and placed a towel down instead.

"You're not going to be comfortable sleeping on that," she explained to Berkley. "If he starts bleeding again, the towel should catch it and there is another plastic sheet between the mattress and the fitted sheet. Why don't ye get some sleep," she suggested. "We're going to get in bed as soon as James locks everything up."

Berkley gingerly climbed over Ian, lying on his side to face him. He placed his hand over Ian's, listening to his breathing as he fell asleep.

'Ber?'

Berkley jolted away. "Wha—?"

'Ian? Are you awake?' Berkley asked, holding his breath as he waited for an answer.

'Sort of. What happened? Are we safe? Did they hurt ye?' Ian asked, fear in his voice. He clearly remembered a gun being pointed at Berkley, but his memories were fuzzy from the pain after he was shot. When he began to struggle to sit up, Berkley gently held him down.

'Stop, love. I'm fine. We're at your parents'. After they shot you, Marco showed up and stopped them from doing anything else. Shaye could feel you were hurt and healed you. The bullet hit your heart, but the magic in the witch's satchel and your bracelet stopped it from going all the way through. I got the bullet out and Shaye healed your heart, a rib bone, and some muscles. She passed out before she could get the wound all the way closed. It was too far of a distance, and she was exhausted. I have it bandaged now and once she's rested, she said she'll finish.'

'I guess the immortality thing worked?' Ian asked.

'You would have died otherwise. Marco made it seem that with the immortality, you would have lived, but recommended getting the bullet out so you wouldn't be weak.'

'Come snuggle,' Ian told him sleepily.

'I don't want to hurt you,' Berkley protested.

'Love, I feel like I got hit by a train. Ye make me feel better, so c'mere,' Ian said, making a grabby hand motion.

'Fine, but you need to drink,' Berkley said, scooting over to spoon his lover. He placed his wrist over Ian's mouth, loving the feel of his fangs sliding into him and drinking. Ian only took a few swallows before licking his wrist and falling back asleep.

Shaye took one final look at where Ian's wound had been. It had been a couple days since the shooting, but it looked great. *'You're all healed; however, you need to eat more, drink more. Your metabolism was already higher, but now it's running crazy high. You're burning through the calories faster than you take them in and you need to replenish what you lost. I want you to try eating something every hour, even if it's a donut or an apple. At this point, I don't care if you eat cookies all day. Well, as long as you also get some meat and vegetables too. You probably need to drink a couple times a day as well. You lost a lot of blood and it's slow coming back, which is why you're so tired. Drink blood, lots of water, maybe some sports drinks. If you ever scare me like that again, I will smack you,'* Shaye threatened.

'I love ye too, piuthar,' Ian responded, knowing she was scolding because she had been scared.

'I love you. No more getting hurt, okay? Gage is working on a way home that doesn't involve flying. With the hunters there, he's worried about the safety of the airport and the flight. He said you have paperwork that they can't get a hold of.'

'How does he know about that?' Ian asked.

'I think Marco said something to him? My guess is Marco would be your way home. He can transport people, but I'm not sure how far. Are you still thinking of coming home about the same time?'

'Probably. Mam is fretting, so I want to give her more time to settle down. Maybe see me with my energy back so she knows I'm okay. At least she and Berkley seem to have bonded, so that's one good thing that came of this. They both like to boss me around and try to get me to eat more.'

'You should listen to them,' Shaye advised.

'Yeah, yeah. I'll do better. I just haven't felt like eating, only sleeping. I think I slept most of the time since the shooting. I wake up when they bring me food or blood but fall asleep right after. Walking to the bathroom feels like taking a strenuous hike. Berkley had to carry me several times because I didn't have the energy to make it back to bed.'

'That's because you don't have enough energy to fuel yourself, or even the blood supply you need yet. It's a bit of a catch-twenty-two; you need to move and eat to get energy, but you need energy to feel like you want to eat. Immortal does not mean invincible. You need to take care of yourself. Eat and drink. I'll check in on you again tomorrow. If you need anything though, promise you'll call me?' Shaye asked. She was worried about Ian. She could tell he had already lost a lot of weight in the couple days since his injury.

'I will. Now go to sleep, I know ye hae work tomorrow,' Ian told her.

'Alright. Love you,' Shaye said.

'Love ye, too.'

Ian looked up as his da' placed a cup in front of him. "Ye need to drink this, all of it. Your mam and I put some in there. You're still weak even though your friend did a great job of healing your injury."

"She just yelled at me too," Ian said with a laugh. "I'll do better."

"Good. Your mam was worried," James said gruffly. "I got your car cleaned out. Ye made a right mess of it, but I used my magic cleaner and got all the bloodstains out. They'll never know what happened."

"Thank ye, Da'."

"Your man seems like a fine gentleman. He's always helping when he can. I think ye've got a winner there," James said, studying his fingernails.

Ian smiled. It's not like he had a big hand in finding his perfect match, Fate had done all the work, but he was glad his da' approved. It seemed all his worrying about bringing home a male partner was for nothing and he couldn't be happier to have been wrong. "Thank ye," he said.

James nodded once. "Now drink your blood. Your mam is going to make some cookies in a bit. Ye need to put some weight on. I hae no idea how ye lost so much in two days."

Ian took his cup and started drinking. He had been spoiled on Berkley's blood, he supposed. His mam and da's didn't taste the same, although it could be because they fed mostly on the farm's livestock instead of human blood.

He felt a familiar brush against his mind. *'Hello, love. Are ye having fun with Mam?'*

'I am. We're collecting eggs,' Berkley replied. *'I'm going to make some deviled eggs when we get in. How does that sound?'*

'They're one of my favorites,' Ian replied, smiling.

'I know. Hopefully they tempt you into eating.'

'Shaye just scolded me about eating as well. It's not like I don't want to…well, I don't want to, I just want to sleep, but she said it's because my blood supply is still low and I'm burning through my calories too fast. I'll do better,' Ian promised.

He hadn't looked at himself yet, not really having the energy to even move far from the bed. How bad could he look?

'Why don't you grab a shower? That normally helps everyone feel better. You don't have a dressing to worry about getting wet anymore. I bet it will feel good,' Berkley suggested.

It wasn't a bad idea; he was feeling a little itchy from where the bandages had been. His da' was puttering around the kitchen, so there would be someone in the house if he got too weak.

"I'm going to grab a shower, Da'," Ian said.

"Let me grab ye a towel," James replied. He hurried to grab a new washcloth and towel, placing them in the bathroom within easy reach of the shower. "Call if ye need help."

Ian shuffled his way to the bathroom. Waiting for the water to heat up, he sat on the toilet, already tired from the short walk. This was ridiculous, he thought. He used to run across whole states in a day. He knew a bullet to the heart should have killed him, but the satchel, bracelet, and Doc's shared immortality had saved him. His body just hadn't gotten the memo yet. Feeling the water had reached the right temperature, he stood and took his clothes off. Glancing at himself in the mirror, he gasped. He had always been lean with defined muscles. Now he looked almost gaunt, several ribs showing. His Adonis belt, the V at his hipbones, was now deeply carved, his hipbones sharp enough to poke someone's eye out which was not sexy. He must have lost at least thirty or more pounds. No wonder everyone kept harping at him to eat. He climbed into the shower, letting the heat work on muscles that had been sore from lying in bed. Oh, it felt nice to be clean. Turning off the shower, he was tired again. Ian wrapped a towel around his waist but didn't get much farther.

'Ber, can you come help me in the bathroom?' Ian asked.

'Of course. Are you hurt, what do you need?'

'No, not hurt. I forgot to bring in clean clothes and I really dinnae want to put on the same clothes I've been in. I think I hae enough energy to make it to the bed, but no' to make it to the suit-

case, get clothes, walk back to the bathroom to change, and then back to the bed,' Ian confessed.

'I'll get your clothes,' Berkley said.

Minutes later, there was a knock on the door. Berkley poked his head in. "I got you some sweatpants and a t-shirt. Do you need help putting them on?"

"Maybe. Can ye make sure I don't tip over?" Ian asked. He put the t-shirt on first, thinking it would be easier. He stayed seated, putting his pants on both legs at the same time, Berkley holding on to his arm as he stood and pulled them up. He was grateful the sweatpants had a drawstring; otherwise his pants would have fallen down.

"I didn't know I looked so bad," Ian admitted.

"Hmm. Did you drink yet?" Berkley asked. He could feel the high vibration Ian's body was still putting out.

"Da' gave me some," Ian said.

"Well, since we have the bathroom to ourselves, why don't you take another couple sips from me," Berkley offered.

"I don't want to make ye weak either," Ian protested. He knew he had been drinking from Berkley much more than normal. He had no desire to cause his mate any harm.

"I'm fine. Just a few more sips," Berkley encouraged. He knew Shaye had recommended eating frequently, so he hoped that having some of his blood would give Ian enough energy to eat another meal or snack when they left the bathroom. Berkley pulled Ian closer, softly kissing his lips before tilting his head. He grinned as Ian bent down, licking his neck before sliding his teeth in. Berkley's cock twitched in interest, even though this was not the time. Of course, normally when Ian was feeding from him, they were having sex. Ian moaned quietly as he took several swallows and then licked the puncture marks closed.

"Thank ye, *mo ghaol*," Ian said, pressing a kiss to Berkley's lips.

"Let's see what your mom has available for a snack,"

Berkley said, knowing he had to get Ian to eat and if they stayed in the bathroom he would be too tempted to follow through with his cock's interest. It had been days since they had been intimate with each other, which considering he used to go hundreds of years without companionship wasn't that long of a time, but his body had woken up when it met Ian.

"Love, are ye alright?" Ian asked quietly, sensing tension in Berkley.

"I'm fine, you're the one who was injured. Now that you're getting better, I'm good. Come on, let's see if I can't get you something to eat while I work on making the deviled eggs." Berkley kissed Ian's cheek, leading him out of the bathroom. He walked slowly, keeping an arm around him. He was not a fan of the rib bones he could feel against his arm. At this rate, Ian's metabolism would eat him down to nothing. Maybe he could make a protein milkshake. It was still cool outside, but Ian was always down for sweets. He could do a berry base with peanut butter for protein and spinach for iron, the ice cream and milk would be good for calcium. If Charlotte didn't have the ingredients, he would run into town the next time Ian took a nap, which would probably be in the next half hour or so.

Sitting Ian at the table, Berkley pulled out some salami and cheese and made a few quick roll-ups. He placed the plate, along with a glass of whole milk in front of Ian.

"Eat. I'm going to get the eggs boiling," Berkley said, kissing the top of Ian's head before heading to the kitchen. He put several of the eggs they had just gotten this morning in a large pot and covered them with water. "Hopefully, I will have them finished for dinner but if not, you'll at least have them for an evening snack. I was thinking of making milkshakes later too. Do you know if your mom has a blender?" Berkley asked. He could mix it by hand, but it was easier to get the spinach pureed in a blender. A food processor might work, he thought. When he didn't get an answer, he turned around. Ian was asleep on the table. Drying his hands off, Berkley walked over and picked up his sleeping man. He carried him over to their bed and laid him down, covering him with a blanket. At least he drank all the milk and ate about half of the roll-ups. Berkley snacked on the remaining ones before washing the plate and looking for milkshake items.

"Is he asleep again?" Charlotte asked, coming inside the house with a new bucket of milk.

Berkley nodded. "He got his shower though and had some blood. I managed to get a cup of milk and some food in him as well. I wanted to make him a milkshake; I'm hoping it entices his appetite to return. I had a few things I wanted to use and was going to run into town to get some supplies. Do you need anything while I'm there?" he asked. He hadn't seen some of the things he needed, and it wasn't fair to keep asking Ian's parents to run to the store. They refused to use the money he gave them, but he knew their income wasn't as good as his or Ian's. If he ran in, he could help with restocking the groceries. He knew they had eaten a lot of their food while they were here.

"I was going to send James later, I have a wee shopping list," she replied.

"I'll get it," Berkley offered. "I'm already going in. Was there anything else besides the list? Post office or anything?"

"Nae, thank ye." Charlotte handed him the list, giving him a kiss on his cheek.

"Thank you for having us. I know this isn't quite what you expected," Berkley replied, giving her a quick hug.

Berkley drove the short distance to town, keeping an eye out for anyone who looked out of place. Parking in front of the grocery store, he hopped out with Charlotte's list.

"Good afternoon," the cashier greeted him.

"Hello," he replied.

"Are ye Charlotte and James' son-in-law?"

"I am," Berkley said. Ah, small towns. He thought Rockfort was small, but this town was so small everyone had no choice but to know everyone else.

"How is Ian? James said he wasn't feeling well when I asked where he had been. I thought he would have stopped in to help his folks with shopping," she asked.

"He's still under the weather. I have Charlotte's list and I was hoping you carried a blender or a food processor? I was hoping to make milkshakes for dessert tonight."

"I love milkshakes. Those cheer anyone up," she agreed. "It must be something bad, if he's still sick. At least it doesn't seem contagious. Let me go see if we hae anything in the back. I can help ye find things if you hae trouble finding some of Charlotte's items."

"Thank you."

Berkley strolled around the small store, picking up items on both lists. He saw a lovely potted plant that was blooming and thought Charlotte would like it, so he placed it in the cart. He couldn't find any frozen fruit, but he bought some fresh bananas and a few different types of berries. He managed to find everything except the blender. He supposed he could always grind up the spinach. Berkley grabbed a few more items that he knew they had depleted during their stay and headed toward the cashier stand.

"I found one left from Christmas in the stock room," she told Berkley, pointing to the dusty blender box.

"That is amazing, thank you!" Berkley said.

"Is the plant for Ian?"

"No, I thought Charlotte might like it. They've been so nice to have us visit," Berkley said.

"Oh, that's nice. James doesn't buy her many flowers, I'm sure she'll love it. How long are ye staying?"

"Just for a few more days," he replied. Berkley paid and hurried out of the store. He was not used to strangers being so nosy.

'Shaye? Are you up?' Berkley asked quietly along the Clan link.

'I am. How are you doing? Are you getting any rest, or have you been too worried about Ian?'

'I'm okay. I'm worried about him though. His metabolism is out of control. He's lost so much weight over just a couple of days. He's burning through calories quicker than he can take them in,' Berkley said.

'I'm not entirely sure why his system went into hyperdrive. Doc and I are trying to figure it out. I'll check on him again and see if I can't convince it to get back to his normal speed, or at least slower than it currently is. Doc's worried that the combination of gaining Doc's immortality and an injury that would have normally killed him, has caused his body to freak out. It's like it's trying to overcompensate but hasn't registered that everything has been healed.'

'Without the added immortality boost, that bullet would have killed him, so I hope Doc doesn't feel bad. My bracelet and the witch's satchel stopped it from going all the way through, but I don't think that would have saved him if he hadn't been immortal as well. He had immortality from me, but the Fae can still be killed, so it's not a true immortality. Maybe Doc's is? I'm honestly not sure, but I'm grateful for whatever combination allowed him to live. I'm going to make him deviled eggs and a protein milkshake. Hopefully that gets him to eat more. I managed to get a little bit of food in him earlier.'

'Okay, I'll scan him again and see if I can't get his system to revert back to normal. We love you guys, stay safe,' Shaye said.

Berkley drove back to the farm. Charlotte and James were sitting in a pair of rocking chairs watching the landscape. He gave them a nod since his hands were full and went inside, putting away groceries and washing the blender. Walking over to Ian, he placed a hand on his chest, letting his magic check on his mate.

'Berkley? How does he seem now?' Shaye asked.

'It's a lot better, thank you. Not quite back to his regular, but a

lot closer,' Berkley replied.

'Okay, good. I'm going to leave it alone for now. I don't want to interfere too much and risk his body freaking out again. I am hoping that it will realize it's okay to slow back down on its own, but if it doesn't start self-regulating by tomorrow night, I'll tweak it again,' Shaye promised.

'Thank you,' Berkley replied, feeling relieved now that Ian's body was slowing down a little.

The door opened and Charlotte came in. "How was the store?" she asked.

"It was good. I found everything on your list," he added. Walking over to the table, he set the bags down and took out the plant, handing it to Charlotte. "Thank you for everything," he said.

"Oh, it's lovely. Thank ye," Charlotte replied, smelling the blooms. "Was Carly there?"

"Uh, I didn't catch her name. Younger girl, nineteen or twenty, blondish hair."

"Yep, that's her. Did she talk your ear off? She's a gossip, that one."

"She certainly asked a lot of questions. Although she did find a blender," he added. "I'm going to make Ian a protein shake, but I thought I could make the rest of us regular milkshakes after dinner. I still need to finish the deviled eggs, but they should be cool enough to work with by now."

"That sounds like a nice treat! I have a roast in the oven with potatoes and carrots for dinner, should be ready in a couple of hours. If ye have time, take a nap," she recommended. "I ken ye didn't get much sleep since Ian was hurt. Ye need to take care of yourself too." She patted his hand before heading back outside.

Berkley put the groceries away before making the deviled eggs and covering them on a plate in the fridge to stay cold. A nap did sound good, he thought, toeing off his shoes and climbing into bed next to Ian.

10

I an woke, stretching his arms and legs toward either end of the bed, groaning as his muscles released their stiff positions. Man, he still felt achy and a little tender everywhere, but so much better than yesterday, or whatever day this was. He rolled to his side, looking at Berkley. He had shadows under his eyes, indicating he hadn't been sleeping well. His poor mate. Ian reached out, gently brushing the few strands of hair that had escaped the braid off Berkley's face. He had taken such good care of Ian when he was healing. It was hard to believe that he had survived being shot in the heart.

He felt a gentle questioning brush against his mind. *'Morning, Shaye. What are ye doing up so early?'* Ian said, reaching out.

'Couldn't sleep. I wanted to make sure you were okay. How are you feeling?' she asked.

'Better, still sore but so much better than before,' Ian replied. *'Berkley looks exhausted though.'*

'Hmm,' Shaye hummed, taking a minute to examine Berkley as well. *'He's just tired, nothing a little more sleep and some food won't fix. I tried to convince your hyperactive metabolism*

to slow down yesterday, so I'm glad it seems to be working. If you notice it ramping back up, give me a call so I can help. Has this happened before when you've been injured, Ian? We can't figure out why your body reacted the way it did. Your metabolism has always been higher than most people, but this was something else.'

Ian took a minute to think. *'I remember getting ridiculously hungry, like hamster hungry, the few times I was badly injured. But nothing to this extent, just a gnawing hunger that seemed to go away as soon as I gorged myself for a little bit. This time, it went straight past that to the point where I wasn't hungry anymore, just tired.'*

'Maybe it was the seriousness of this injury, or the new immortality combined with the injury, I just don't know,' Shaye said, frustrated. *'If anything like this happens again, I'm shoving blood and food down your throat as soon as I get the injury healed. Maybe even a feeding tube if you won't eat,'* she threatened. *'You scared all of us. I was so worried that the bullet wouldn't kill you, but your own stupid body would.'*

'I wasn't trying to be difficult,' Ian swore.

'Well, be extra nice to Berkley and let him fuss over you if he wants. I know you like being independent and you're "Mr. I Do It Myself," but he was really worried.'

'I'll let him give me a sponge bath if he wants to,' he teased.

'TMI, Ian. Unless you want me to share too?' Shaye shot back.

Ian gagged; nope, he did not want to hear what his little sister got up to. It was bad enough when he walked by their door and caught any sounds. *'NO!'* he squawked. *'I'm good.'*

'Okay. Take it easy today, make sure to keep your food and blood consumption up for at least a few more days. I'm going to go make some coffee and get ready for work. Love you,' Shaye said.

'Love ye too,' Ian replied.

Ian pulled the curtain back a little bit, listening for any sounds of movement. It seemed like everyone was still asleep. He grabbed his phone from the shelf and checked the time. Huh, it was almost nine, it was odd his parents were still asleep. He slid out of bed, grabbing a towel on his way to the bathroom. His legs no longer felt wobbly, like he could collapse at any time. His face had moved from scruff to scraggly beard starting. He had never been able to grow a good beard; he wasn't sure if that was genetics or being turned at eighteen. Standing in the shower, he let the hot water run over him, the heat and steam helping his muscles. He bent over, touching his toes, letting the muscles stretch before placing his hands flat on the shower floor. He groaned slightly, oh that felt good.

Getting out of the shower, Ian dried off, wrapping the towel around his waist to brush his teeth and to wrestle his hair into submission. It felt so good to shave the scruff off. He took a good look at himself in the mirror, noting that his face looked a little better, not as gaunt. His torso was still much too thin, but it didn't look like it had gotten any worse. Shaye really helped getting his metabolism under control. He actually felt a little hungry and still had energy after the shower. Go him. Making breakfast for everyone would be nice, he thought as he threw on an everyday kilt and a sweater. Might as well be comfortable and his pants were hanging a little loosely right now. He was glad that his kilt had room for adjustment using the buckles. Wandering out to the kitchen, he opened the fridge to see what was available. Ooo, bacon sounded good. It didn't look like the eggs had been collected yet, so he shoved his feet in his boots and went in search of fresh eggs. He moved slowly, but so far, his body was holding up. The chickens were certainly happy to see him, coming over to see if he had any food. He tossed out some feed, keeping them busy while he gathered the eggs. He set the pail off to the side, stopping to feed the other animals and to milk the cow.

Stepping inside the house, he placed the milk and eggs down before removing his boots. He grabbed the double boiler and set up the milk on the stove. As a vampire, he probably didn't need to pasteurize the milk, but it was what he was used to. He set the eggs in the sink to wash off as well.

"It helps if you light the stove, son," his mam said dryly behind him.

"I forgot it was wood burning," he admitted, turning to give her a kiss on the cheek.

"I'll grab some kindling and get it going," Charlotte said, sliding her feet into her house slippers. "What are ye making?"

"Bacon and eggs. I was hungry and thought I'd make breakfast for everyone," Ian replied.

"That sounds good. Your da' and I were up late playing cards with Berkley. I'm no' used to sleeping in this late. Did ye feed the animals while ye were out there?"

"Yes, Mam. What games did ye play?"

"Crazy Eights, Rummy, a bit of poker."

"Ye played poker?" Ian asked incredulously.

"It was fun."

"Okay then. Maybe we can play something after breakfast?" He never thought he'd see the day when his mam played poker. She had never wanted to learn, saying gambling was a waste, even though he told her you didn't have to gamble if you were playing for fun.

After his mam lit the oven, Ian placed the bacon strips on a cooking sheet so that it could bake in the oven. The stovetop only had a few burners, which were already claimed by the milk, the eggs, and the tea kettle. Filling the kettle, he got the water started, knowing his mam liked a cup of tea first thing in the morning. He missed his coffee though. He had bought his parents a French press years ago so he could have a cup when he came to visit, but he had forgotten to bring coffee with them. His mam and da' had never really jumped on the coffee trend, preferring their tea.

Ian poured two cups of tea, going out to sit on the porch

with his mam. The bacon needed about fifteen minutes and then he would get the eggs scrambled up.

"Here, Mam," Ian said, handing the cup over before sitting.

"Thank ye," Charlotte replied, smiling. She sat there quietly for a few minutes, enjoying the quiet and the opportunity to sit with her only child. "I like your man," she said. "He's such a nice boy. A little quiet, but it probably wouldn't work if ye both were as talkative as ye. He clearly loves ye, which is all I could ever want in a partner for ye."

Ian swallowed the laugh that threatened to ruin the moment. He didn't think his mam realized Berkley was older than she was. "He is and he does. I love him too. We balance each other, I think. I couldn't ask for a better mate, Fate did a great job."

"He's no' bad to look at either," his mam said with a side-eyed smirk.

"That he is," Ian agreed. "I've never seen eyes like his, that purple-blue color." Berkley was a little shorter than Ian, but he was the perfect kissing height.

"Where's he from?" Charlotte asked. She wanted to know more about her son's partner, but with Berkley being quieter than Ian, she hadn't wanted to push too much. They had been getting on well and she didn't want to accidentally bring something up that would cause problems or upset him. She didn't know a lot about his background.

"England. He's from a Fae colony there. It's set back in these dense woods; apparently, it's warded so that non-Fae cannae find it. The Fae are an odd bunch, I think. Berkley says it's common practice for them to be very reserved, even among their own families. That they love each other, but don't show it well. No' a lot of hugs and kisses it seems like. He's gotten better being around the Clan, as some of us are rather touchy."

"Uh huh," his mam agreed, looking straight at him.

Ian laughed. He was a touchy sort of person. Everyone got a hug. Pre-mate days, if you were cute, there would be lots of extra little touches. Nothing outwardly sexual just in case the other person wasn't interested, but brushing a hand over their hair, fingers running over their arm or back, sitting close enough to feel the heat from each other's bodies. Physical touch was a big thing with Ian, and although it wasn't with Berkley, his mate always made an effort to give him what he needed. It had been a little awkward in the beginning, like Berkley patting his back or the one time he linked arms for some reason instead of holding hands. But it had all been sweet, all efforts to let Ian know he was wanted and loved. Ian in turn tried to not be such a slob in their bedroom, something that drove Berkley nuts. He liked things clean and in their place, so Ian made an effort to always put things back where they belonged, not to leave socks or towels on the floor. Sometimes it was the little everyday things that made a big difference. Although it would be a bit of a relief to have their workshop built, he thought. It was hard to keep everything as tidy as Berkley liked it while Ian was working on a project. He tended to get lost in it and clean-up usually happened at the end. If they both had their own side, he thought that would make them both happier. Berkley's could be kept spotless, and Ian's could be a little messier, although he would still try to clean up at the end of the day instead of at the end of the project.

"By the way, son. When did ye get those little bars? I hae to say, seeing your nipples pierced came as quite the surprise," his mam said dryly, taking a sip of her tea.

The timer went off on Ian's phone for the bacon. "Oh, look at that! I'm going to go make the eggs. I'll put the kettle on for more tea," he told his mam. He had forgotten that he hadn't had his nipples pierced the last time he was here. When he went inside, the curtain was pulled back on his parents' bed and the shower was running. Scrambling the eggs, he poured his da' a cup of tea when he heard the shower shut off.

"Weel, look who's up! You're looking better," his da' said, patting him on the back.

"Thanks, Da'. I'm feeling a lot better," Ian said. "Do ye mind putting on some clothes? I'm going to wake Berkley for breakfast."

His da' looked down at himself in surprise before barking out a laugh. "I'm so used to running around letting my bits air dry a bit after a shower, I forgot to bring my clothes. I'll get some on."

"When did ye start doing that?" Ian asked. He definitely would have remembered his da' running around in the buff.

"Eh, sometime after ye moved out. I'd been trying my best to remember while ye are here, but I'm off schedule today."

As soon as his da' pulled some pants on, Ian turned the eggs off and went over to his bed.

"Good morning, love," he said quietly, kissing Berkley on the forehead. "Breakfast is almost ready."

Berkley grumbled something but reached out a hand and pulled Ian back into the bed, tucking him in against him. "Snuggles," Berkley muttered.

Ian laughed softly. It looked like his touchiness was rubbing off on his mate. "Come on, love. Eggs and bakey!"

Sleepy eyes cracked open, slowly blinking at him. "Bacon?"

"Mhm, bacon and scrambled eggs," Ian replied, rubbing his nose against Berkley's.

"Ian!" Berkley shot up, almost knocking into Ian's head. "You're up!" he exclaimed, his voice cracking as he dragged Ian into a hug. Oh gods, the overwhelming relief to see his mate up and looking a little better. Grabbing Ian's face, he pulled him in and pressed a kiss to his lips.

"Shh, I'm fine. Shaye already gave me a check-up this morning. It looks like whatever she did helped my body get back to its normal rhythm." Ian held Berkley tight, feeling the slight vibrations in his muscles as he tucked his head into Ian's neck. "I'm alright, love," he said softly. He heard his da' go out to the front porch to give them some privacy.

'*I was worried,*' Berkley said, holding on tight.

'*Ye took such good care of me. Thank ye,*' Ian replied, pressing a kiss against Berkley's head.

'*You should eat,*' Berkley told him, pulling back to look at Ian. His face and body were still too thin, but it hadn't gotten any worse which made him very happy.

'*Food is ready now,*' Ian replied, tilting his head in confusion.

Berkley reached out and pulled Ian's head to his neck. '*You should eat,*' he repeated.

Ian licked their favorite spot, Berkley's claiming mark, loving the shudder that went through the other man. He could feel both of their cocks stirring and wondered just how long his parents would stay outside. '*Ye have to be quiet,*' Ian warned, licking the spot again, causing Berkley to gasp. He fished Berkley's cock out of his pants and tucked his kilt up to press his own shaft against it. Fisting them both together, he slid his teeth into Berkley's neck, pressing his free hand to Berkley's mouth when he let out a low moan. It didn't take them long, the relief of Ian's recovery and being together again causing them to cum quickly. Ian licked Berkley's neck, closing the skin. Berkley pulled off his t-shirt to clean them up.

'*Thank ye,*' Ian said, giving him one last kiss before climbing out of the bed and adjusting his kilt. "I'm going to wash up and I'll get the food plated."

Berkley nodded. "I'll go brush my teeth and get changed."

As soon as the bathroom door shut, his mam poked her head in, shaking her head at him. "All clear to come in?"

"Yup," Ian said with an unrepentant grin.

"Did ye wash your hands?" his mom asked, her lips twitching as she tried not to smile.

"Mam!" Ian whisper-shouted. "Yes, I did."

They had one more full day left in Scotland. Ian wanted to show Berkley one of his favorite spots when he was a kid. He packed a picnic lunch and they drove to the nearby loch. Normally they would walk, but after the run-in with the hunters, he wanted the safety of the vehicle instead of the forty-five-minute walk, most of which was through open fields that didn't provide a lot of cover. Pulling up to the loch, Ian looked out over the water with its gray shores, the water gently carving patterns into the shore. Various-sized rocks were scattered about, giving them an option of where to sit. They ate their lunch, watching as the birds dove for their own meal. It was peaceful today, even a little warm out. Berkley was searching through the smaller stones along the shore, so Ian took their lunch remains back to the car. Last night, he had found the inflatable sheep he had bought their first day in Scotland. He grinned to himself as he quickly blew it up, keeping an ear out for the sounds of his mate. He tossed it in the back seat, strapping the middle seat belt around it and managed to get the door shut before Berkley came over.

"I found some neat stones," Berkley said, showing Ian a handful of rocks. "I think if I polish this one up, it will look great in a bracelet or pendant."

Ian took a closer look. "I think so too. It has some great colors and pattern. You ready to go?"

Berkley nodded. "I still have to finish packing," he replied.

They climbed in the car and were soon bouncing along the dirt road. "Ian. Why is there an inflatable sheep in the back seat?" Berkley asked, not sure if he really wanted to know the answer.

"Weel, I saw the wee lass back in Edinburgh and couldn't resist," Ian replied. "She's no' my type really, but she wanted to come along anyway."

"Not your...is that a sex toy?" Berkley asked, scandalized.

Ian looked at Berkley, seeing the horror on his face. He started laughing so hard he had to stop the car.

"It's not funny!" Berkley protested. "You bought an inflatable sex toy...I...why...I don't even..."

"It's a novelty item, love. Just for fun. Not sexy fun, ha-ha fun. I just wanted to see your face," Ian admitted.

Berkley got a look on his face that Ian couldn't interpret. Whipping out his phone, he snapped a picture and quickly typed out a message.

"What're ye doing?" Ian asked curiously.

"I'm telling Shaye," Berkley replied smugly.

"No! She'll tell Tess and I'll never hear the end of sheep jokes!" Ian protested, even though he was secretly pleased Berkley had gotten so comfortable with everyone that he was sharing sex jokes.

"You should have thought of that before," Berkley replied primly. He was making plans to subtly bring sheep up for the next several weeks.

Ian pulled into his parents' drive. His da' was coming out of the barn and came over to greet them. He did a double take when he saw the back seat.

"Ian. Son. Why do ye have a sheep in the back seat?"

"It was a joke, Da'," Ian replied.

"Right. Weel, if ye aren't bringing it home, ye can leave it here," James suggested, leering at the sheep.

Ian felt his nose scrunch up in disgust. "What? No. Ew, Dad!"

James burst out laughing, Berkley joining in. Ian reached into the back seat and grabbed the sheep. Pulling out the stopper, it began to deflate.

"Dinnae ye want to show your mam your new friend?" James gasped out, still laughing.

"It's no' my—it was a joke. I just wanted to see Berkley's face," Ian tried explaining again.

"Sure, son. Whatever ye say." James patronizingly patted Ian's back. "C'mon Berkley, ye can hang out wi' me if Ian doesn't appreciate ye."

Berkley gave Ian a quick wink and a grin before following James. Ian never would have guessed his da' would have joined in on the joke, much less take it even further and turn it around on him. He was happy though; it meant his parents were easing up a bit. Plus, his mam and da' seemed to really hit it off with Berkley. They must have bonded a lot when he was injured. He folded the plastic up, making sure to get all the air out. At this point, he was going to have to stuff it down in his suitcase and hide it from his mam. Berkley had already sent a picture to at least Shaye, so he supposed he would just bring it home. He could have it randomly show up in different rooms of the house, he thought, grinning. Kind of like that elf thing at Christmas, but not as creepy looking. Well, maybe not as creepy looking.

"Hi, Mam," he called out as he walked into the house. "Da' stole my mate. Did ye need any help wi' dinner or anything?"

"I'm making some cookies for dessert, could ye see if there are any eggs in the coop?" Charlotte asked, her head inside the fridge.

"Sure," Ian replied. He took the opportunity to shove the deflated sheep down to the bottom of his suitcase.

It was finally time to go back home. Marco was going to teleport them to the Clan estate, and they had arranged to meet him at the farm for pick up. If he meant them any harm, he wouldn't be able to get through the wards. They were also leaving at night, giving them better coverage if someone was nearby. It would be hard to see them suddenly disappear in the dark. They should get home about dinnertime.

Marco met them near the SUV. "I can bring this back to the rental car place so your parents don't have to deal with it, if you would like?"

"That would be great," Ian said. "Thanks. Mam and Da' don't like traveling that far, so I was a little worried about how we were going to get it back."

"I'll drop that off and then I'll be right back for you guys," Marco replied.

He grabbed the key, sat in the driver's seat, and then they both just vanished. His mam gasped. "Weel, that's certainly something. I had no idea someone could do that."

"I've only heard of Marco doing it. We only knew about it because Tess saw him take the guys who attacked her and Sam. I don't think it's very common," Berkley answered.

It was less than a minute later when Marco popped back in. "Sorry, the door on the key drop box was finicky. It took me a little longer than I thought. You have everything you need?"

Ian looked around; they had both their suitcases and carry-on bags. They had made sure the souvenirs and papers from the festival were in Berkley's bag that had been spelled. "I think so."

"Okay. Grab your bags in one hand and then each of you take one of my hands. It's going to feel weird, but don't let go or I have no idea where you'll end up."

Ian looked at him to see if he was joking, but the man had a serious face on. He had only met him in person today, he didn't count the day he was attacked, and he couldn't tell if he was pulling their leg or not. He glanced over at Berkley who gave him a small shrug.

Charlotte came over, looking a little nervous. "Call me when ye get home?"

Ian leaned down and gathered his mam in a hug. "I will. Thank ye for having us, I missed ye."

James gave Berkley a hug. "Come back soon. I don't ken where we'd put them but bring some of your friends next time too. We'd like to meet them."

Ian nodded. "We will. Shaye wants to meet ye," he replied, getting his own back-thumping hug from his da'.

Charlotte grabbed Berkley in a hug, giving him a kiss on the cheek. "It was so nice meeting ye. Ye are the perfect partner for Ian. Now, he's no' the best at keeping us in the loop, so if anything big happens, make sure to tell us. Alright?"

"I will," Berkley promised. He already had plans to buy them a cell phone and have it delivered to their house. He was going to find a service that would both deliver and show them how to use their phones. Berkley didn't want to add any expenses for Ian's parents, so he was going to pay for their phone plan. With Ian and his parents reconnecting so well, he thought that they would love getting text messages and pictures. It would help them stay connected a little more, plus they could see what everyone looked like and feel like they were a part of their lives.

"I think we're ready," Ian said, looking at Marco. He saw Berkley had changed his carry-on bag with the papers to act as a crossbody bag, making sure it wouldn't slip off his shoulder and get lost. Berkley gave Ian a kiss and then grabbed Marco's hand, squeezing tight. Ian shook his head; Marco probably shouldn't have mentioned getting lost in transport. Berkley was probably terrified since he hated flying and had no way of knowing what this would feel like. Ian grabbed his bag in one hand, Marco's hand in the other.

"By—" Ian started to say, but there was a jolting sensation, and he could hear Berkley gasp. It seemed like a blink of an eye, and they were suddenly standing just inside of the Clan house gates.

"Sorry, your mom had tears in her eyes. I don't do well with tears," Marco said gruffly. "Anyway, here you are. Keep those things safe. Gage is worried about hunters being in the area, but we haven't been able to track them down yet. There were a few suspicious campsites in the park where camping isn't allowed, but we haven't found any people yet. The wards at the house and your businesses are great, they wouldn't be able to get past those. The Sheriff's office and the backroom at the library are also good spots if you run into trouble in town. I'm off to investigate some other hunter reports, but Gage will keep me up to date," Marco told them.

"Did you find anything about that necklace the hunters had in Scotland? They said it found demons, which we clearly aren't. I think it detects paranormals, but I have no idea how they would have gotten such an item. I can't imagine a paranormal making and giving human hunters one, even if they were paranormals hunting other paranormals," Berkley said.

"No, I'd imagine not," Marco replied. "Human hunters would be more likely to kill than to capture. Paranormal hunters would want people alive, I would think. None of us are any use to people dead. I'm looking into it, it's not the only one I've come across. I haven't been able to track down the source yet. It could be someone who has a gift who was raised human with hunters and somehow created them, or they were stolen, or they bought them. I just don't know yet. Every lead I've had has ended up being a dead end.

"Before I forget, here are your hospital discharge papers. I created a police report that shows you were shot in the shoulder and you both were transported to the local hospital. You were discharged and recovered at home. The local police report will also show that you had to request that your rental car be returned for you, as you were unable to drive it due to your injury. Your return flight home will register that you checked in and boarded the plane. If anyone looks into it further, the memory of your parents dropping you off at the airport will pop up. I wanted to make sure you were covered in the event someone starts digging into the disappearance of the men who attacked you. There was the brother who was there and left; I don't want him thinking you had the means or opportunity to get revenge for your attack and come looking for you," Marco explained, handing them a folder of paperwork.

"I used the rental car to get groceries in town," Berkley told him.

"If anyone asks about it, memories will be changed a little to remember you driving his parents' truck. As a rule, I don't like to mess with anyone's mind, so this will only be triggered in the event of someone asking about you or anything about your trip. It includes conversations, telephone calls, emails, text messages, written letters, anything. It won't affect your parents, Gage or myself, or your Clan.

"I am not liking the increase in hunters lately. If we can't figure this out soon, Gage may need to put protections around the town and the woods to keep the hunters out, but he'll probably need help. It'd be a huge undertaking. In the meantime, you may want to add a concealment spell to your pendants. That way if hunters are in the area with one of those detectors, they won't pick up on you. You want to word it so that it conceals you from evil intentions, but not from everyone. It's hard to help a fellow paranormal if they're registering as human or are blank," Marco added.

Berkley nodded. "I'll get with Tess and see if we can figure something out. Thank you for the transportation. It's much better than flying," he added with a smile.

Marco laughed. "You're welcome. Glad you're better," he directed at Ian. "See ya later." He disappeared.

Ian and Berkley glanced at each other, still amazed that he

could do that. They grabbed their bags and walked up the driveway.

"It's good to be home," Berkley said, drawing in a deep breath.

"It is," Ian agreed. He heard the front door open, Shaye running down the drive.

"You're home!" she said, grabbing them both in a hug. They put their bags down to return the hug. "How are you feeling? Come inside, tell me all about it. I want to check on your wound. Emma has food cooking, it's almost ready. You need to eat. Come on, let's go," she said, trying to drag them up the driveway.

"Slow down," Ian said with a laugh. "We hae to get our bags. It's nice to be home. It was a much faster trip back than flying. Like seconds fast. I ate before we left, but I'm sure I can eat something more."

Berkley grabbed both of their suitcases and carry-ons. *'I'm going to bring these in. You calm her down; she's a little overwhelmed.'* He gave Shaye a kiss as he headed into the house. Rolf was standing at the door and he reached out to grab some of the bags.

"Welcome home. She's been worried, even though she knew he had healed," Rolf said, tipping his head toward Shaye.

"It's one thing to know it, but another to see it and really believe it," Berkley agreed.

"He was her only real family for a long time, before Tess and the rest of us. But I think she never really thought about losing Ian before and it knocked her for a loop."

"Are her mugs here?" Berkley asked. Rolf nodded. "I'll get her a cup of tea, chamomile I think, no caffeine."

Rolf laughed. "No caffeine," he agreed. "She's been up since two this morning and has had enough caffeine to last several days." He followed Berkley in, bringing all their luggage up to their room as Berkley headed toward the kitchen.

Ian took Shaye's hand and held it to his chest, right over where the bullet went in. Her eyes filled with tears that he could see she was desperately fighting not to let fall. "I'm fine, see? No more wound, ye healed me right up. I'm just a wee bit skinny at the moment, but it's much better than before. Ye helped, even across an ocean. I'm here and I'm fine," he stressed, gathering her into a hug.

"But I almost lost you," she protested, sniffing. "You're my family and some jackass almost took you from me."

"It's alright. We know how to protect ourselves, huh? Berkley is going to brainstorm with Tess to figure out a concealment spell to add to our pendants to prevent any hunters from detecting us. The immortality worked; even a bullet didn't kill me. Marco made it sound like I would hae lived, just weak and with a bullet stuck in me. Now that I'm thinking about it, it's weird; we all ken that the Fae's immortality doesn't mean that they can't be killed, so how would he ken that the bullet wouldn't kill me? I should hae been dead, even with the immortality I got from mating with Berkley. So how did he ken a bullet wouldn't kill me? None of us have said anything about the ceremony with Doc, so I'm not sure if or how he would ken about Doc's immortality, but it was a weird statement to make." Of course, with his crazy metabolism in high gear, he didn't know how that would have worked out in the long run either. Would he have just kept wasting away, but never dying? Ian bent his head to rest atop Shaye's, surrounding her with himself. He could feel the tears wetting his shirt, but there wasn't any sound escaping her.

They stood there for several minutes until he felt the tears slow down. "Now, tell me everything I missed," he said.

"They finally named the puppy," Shaye said, loosening her grip a little bit.

"Yeah? What did they name him?"

"Rockefeller. Rock for short," Shaye said with a laugh. "He has started moving around and always seems to end up in a precarious spot, no matter how many times we try to puppy-proof."

"That's a different name. I can't wait to see how much he's grown. Ber and I finally came up with a design for the workshop, I think. I also tried a new thing: metal flowers. I think they would go over well for Valentine's Day and Mother's Day," he added.

"I bet they would," Shaye agreed, finally stepping back and wiping her eyes. "Sorry for crying all over you," she said, trying to wipe down Ian's shirt.

He laughed. "It's fine, little sister. Let's go eat. Did Emma make any cookies?"

Shaye rolled her eyes. "I did. Shortbread and cocoa oatcakes."

"You do love us," Ian exclaimed.

"Duh. Plus, I need to fatten you up. You're still too thin."

Ian held out his arm like a proper gentleman, causing Shaye to laugh. She linked her arm with his and they walked inside where he could hear everyone gathered in the kitchen. He could also smell a lovely stew and soda bread. His stomach grumbled as they walked in the room, causing his mate to laugh at him.

"Hungry?" Berkley asked.

"I wasn't until I smelled the stew," Ian protested. "Shaye said there were cookies too."

Emma looked up from stirring the pot on the stove. "Everything's ready if you all want to grab a bowl. It's a lamb and beef vegetable stew." She grinned at Ian.

Ian groaned, his face pinkening. "Really, Emma?"

She laughed. "Well, Shaye showed us the picture Berkley sent us, and I just couldn't resist. Don't worry, I'm sure everyone won't tease you about it. Much. Now, go sit down.

There's jam and butter at the table already, I just need to finish slicing the bread and I'll bring it out," Emma said, giving Ian a kiss on the cheek. "I'm so glad you're home safely."

Ian sat next to Berkley, allowing the sounds of his family to wash over him. It was good to be home, despite any sheep jokes that might be coming his way.

NOTE FROM THE AUTHOR

Thank you for reading *Forged In Love*! If you enjoyed the story, please leave a review. Reviews, no matter how short, are invaluable to independent authors. Thank you to everyone who leaves reviews!

Keep reading for a sneak peek into *Linked In History*, book five of the Nightwood Clan series. This book will focus on Merri and Gawain.

After the Sneak Peek, you will find a character list in the back of the book as well.

Thank you to the **Artist-Blacksmith's Association of North America** for answering my question on if I could make a propane forge tank explode! It turned out that it wasn't very likely, so Ian ended up cutting himself on his blade instead.

SNEAK PEEK

The next book in the series will be Merri and Gawain's story, *Linked In History*.

Gawain and Doc were holed up in the library, the documents that Ian and Berkley brought home spread out over the old mahogany table. It was a good thing the table was large enough to seat the whole family, as the documents took up a large portion of the tabletop. They each had their own notepads, not wanting to write on originals.

Gawain had been poring over these for days, and his hair was a tangled mess from running his hands through it. These documents were nothing short of amazing. There were secrets galore on them and he had never been more thankful that his friends had enough magic to keep them safe. Something like this in the hands of the hunters could cause irreparable damage. There were species of shifters listed on here that he had never heard of. Although, he supposed it did make sense that Nessie was a shifter. He had always wondered but had never spent enough time in Scotland to really dig into it.

Maybe he should encourage Ian and Shaye's idea of taking a Clan vacation. It could be fun, and he would have an excuse to try to find Nessie. Or whatever the shifter's name might be.

Doc gasped from the other end of the table.

"Gawain! Look at this," he said excitedly.

Gawain jumped up and rushed over, peering over Doc's shoulder to see what he had found. Doc was wearing cotton gloves to keep any oils or residues from his skin from getting on the parchment. He pointed to a section about midway down the page. It looked like it might be in Latin...no... maybe Greek? The handwriting was horrible. He stared at it longer, trying to make sense of it. He read many languages, but damned if this one wasn't making sense to him.

"I can't make it out, Doc. What language is that?"

Doc looked up at him funny. "What do you mean? It's in Greek."

"Doc, I can read Greek. That is not Greek. I can't make out any of the words," Gawain told him, squinting and tilting his head, trying to make sense of the scribbles.

"Really?"

Gawain nodded. Nope, nothing.

"Merri, come look at this!" Gawain shouted.

A minute later, his mate walked in. "You rang?" she asked, exasperation in her voice. She had been enjoying a nice cup of tea and a book in the living room.

"Can you read this?"

Merri walked over to the table, looking over Doc's other shoulder. "No. No, I cannot. Are those even words?"

Doc looked at both of them, frustration on his face. "Are you putting me on?"

Merri shook her head. "Honest, I can't make out a single word. You can read it?"

He nodded. "It's about rare shifters, the ones with immortality. It goes on to say they can claim their families, share their life gift, and their immortality is true immortality. I need to go through the rest of these documents and see if there is anything to back this up."

Gawain nodded. "I'll set aside any documents that don't make sense to me and see if you can read them. Maybe we should have Tess or Berkley see if there is a spell over them, because I'm not sure why we wouldn't be able to read it otherwise."

"That's a good idea," Doc replied. He grabbed his phone and sent off a quick text. Berkley came in a few minutes later, holding a cup of tea.

"You wanted me to look at something?" he asked. "Tess is…um…upstairs…with Sam. So, it's just me for now."

Doc bit his lip to keep from smiling at Berkley, whose face was a nice shade of red. "Can you read this?" he asked, pointing at the document.

Berkley leaned over, his hair falling forward before he leaned back and grabbed a tie out of his pocket to pull it into a ponytail. "I cannot," he replied. "Hmm, well that's interesting," he said, looking at it. He held a hand over the top of it, concentrating. "I didn't sense this when we brought the packet home. There's definitely a spell over the document, almost like a type of concealment spell from what I can sense. Can anyone read it?"

"Merri and I couldn't, but Doc could," Gawain replied.

"Hmm. Have you come across any others?" Berkley asked.

They shook their heads no.

"What does it say?" Berkley asked, looking at Doc.

"It was talking about rare shifters, forming a bond, sharing immortality. It seemed like it was a true immortality, not like the immortality we normally associate with paranormals where they can still be killed in some way."

"Like the Fae," Berkley responded. His species was immortal so long as someone didn't do anything too drastic like lose a head or destroy their heart. They were much harder to kill, but there were still ways to do it. Other paranormals had a natural lifespan where they would stop aging for a while. When it got closer to the end of their life, they would begin to age again. The Fae simply stopped aging, living forever unless mortally wounded.

"Yes," Doc said. "I'm hoping I can find something else in here to help collaborate it. It would be nice knowing how protected you all are now that you have my immortality."

Gawain started zoning out, finding a new document to read through. He would let them talk about spells and whatnot until they came up with an answer. Merri was probably still listening too, but there was something more in this pile calling out to him. It was just like when he was on a dig. If there was something to discover, he had a knack for finding it. The antiques buried in the ground sometimes called to him. He had a feeling that there was something in the pile that would help him with his plans for the dig he was planning when he found Doc's old tribe home. Doc had marked on a map the different places the tribe had lived. The first site they were going to was the one Doc had lived at the longest, the settlement that he had been kicked out of when he was an adult. Gawain just couldn't understand how someone could kick out such an amazing person, not to mention Doc's shifter side. Seriously, who got rid of an alicorn?

They had plans to travel in the late spring or early summer to scout out the area and Merri had already let Marge know she would be taking a break from the library. Gawain couldn't wait to get his hands in the dirt again.

Merri glanced over at her mate, realizing he had zoned out on them. She shook her head. He was on a mission. "Berkley, are you positive you didn't notice anything weird about the documents when you got them?"

He shook his head. "Honestly, it was a bit of a whirlwind. The woman gave them to us, Ian hid them under his sweater, we walked down the aisle to give her time to pack up, and then we were attacked in the parking lot. When we got to Ian's parents' house, I put them in my luggage with an invisibility and protection spell. I was so distracted with getting Ian better, that I didn't really pay much attention to them. Nothing stood out, not even when I gave them to you."

"Do you still have the bag, Doc?" Merri asked.

Doc nodded, handing it over. Merri skimmed it with her magic. "I don't sense anything on the bag either. Do you?" she asked Berkley.

Berkley looked at it, flipping it inside out. "No, nothing. I can't even be sure if she cast the spell over these to keep them from the hunters before giving them to us, or if the spell is much older than that."

Gawain looked up, holding another document. "I found another one!" He passed it over to Doc.

Berkley moved down to the other side of the table, running his hands over the papers there. Nothing. Nothing at all. There was no magic, no spell, nothing his senses could pick up. It was bizarre. He picked up a few of the papers, skimming them. Nothing jumped out, nothing changed until he reached an older piece of parchment. As soon as he looked at it, he felt a spell activate, the words becoming garbled. "I found one as well," he said. "I didn't sense any spells when I came over, but as soon as I looked at this one, something activated and now I cannot read it." He handed it down to Doc.

NIGHTWOOD CLAN

LOCATION

The series is mainly set in Rockfort, Tennessee, a fictional town.

CHARACTERS

Rolfston
Species: Vampire
Mate: Shaye
Job: Investments, day trading, Clan leader
Special Abilities: Telepathy, shielding
Book: Bite Me Again

Shaye
Species: Human/Vampire
Mate: Rolf
Job: Nurse
Special Abilities: Healing
Book: Bite Me Again

Sam

Species: Werewolf
Mate: Tess
Job: Owner, Black Wolf Brewery
Rolf's friend
Book: A Hairy Situation

Tess

Species: Witch
Mate: Sam
Job: Medical coding, nurse
Shaye's friend
Book: A Hairy Situation

Emma (Emmaline)

Species: Vampire
Mate: Doc (Albert)
Job: Landowner/small farm
Special Abilities: Visions/Premonitions
Rolfston's mother
Book: Pointed Love

Doc (Albert)

Species: Alicorn
Mate: Emma
Job: Doctor
Special Abilities: Some healing, visions, magic,
*   immortality*
Book: Pointed Love

Ian
Species: Vampire
Mate: Berkley
Job: Leathersmith, blacksmith
Special Abilities: Speed
Shaye's friend
Book: Forged In Love

Berkley
Species: Fae
Mate: Ian
Job: Owner/Potter, The Winged Potter
*Special Abilities: Can sense auras and species, slight
    healing ability*
Rolf's friend
Book: Forged In Love

Gawain
Species: Falcon shifter
Mate: Merri
Job: Historian/archeologist
Rolf's friend

Merri (Meredith)
Species: Witch
Mate: Gawain
Job: Librarian
Tess's sister

Vladimir
Species: Vampire
Evil father of Rolfston
Note: Appeared in Bite Me Again

Sheriff (Gage)
Species: Unknown
Mate: None (yet)
Job: Sherriff of Rockfort, Warden
Special Abilities: Very strong magic

Duncan
Species: Dragon
Note: Vlad killed his sister. Assisted in battle in Bite Me Again.

Sherri
Species: Human
Job: Receptionist at Doc's clinic

Marge
Species: Cat shifter
Job: Librarian in Rockfort

Marco
Species: Unknown
Job: Hunter for Wardens
Note: Collected the bodies of the men who attacked Tess and Sam. Appeared in A Hairy Situation.

Beth
Species: Human
Mate: Josh (witch)
Job: Florist/Owner, Rockfort Blooms

Samantha
Species: Brownie
Job: Caretaker for Emma's farm in England, weaves and quilts blankets
Note: Mentioned in Pointed Love

Douglas
Species: Gnome
Job: Ferrier, Sculptor, helps on Emma's farm
Note: Mentioned in Pointed Love

Thalia
Species: Unicorn
Job: Healer
Note: Deceased. Mentioned in Pointed Love.

Jacob
Species: Human
Mate: Terrance (bear)
Job: Farmhand
Note: Emma's friend, deceased. Mentioned in
     Pointed Love.

Terrance (Ter)
Species: Bear shifter
Mate: Jacob
Note: Deceased. Mate to Emma's friend Jacob (mated
     in afterlife).

Charlotte
Species: Vampire
Note: Ian's mom. Mentioned in Forged In Love.
James
Species: Vampire
Note: Ian's dad. Mentioned in Forged In Love.

Aggie (Agnes)
Species: Vampire
Note: Ian's aunt. Mentioned in Forged In Love.

Robert
Species: Vampire
Note: Ian's uncle-in-law. Mentioned in Forged In
    Love.

Clara
Species: Vampire
Note: Ian's cousin. Mentioned in Forged In Love.

George
Species: Vampire
Mate: Matthew
Note: Robert's brother. Mentioned in Forged in
    Love.

Matthew
Species: Vampire
Mate: George
Note: Mentioned in Forged in Love.

ABOUT THE AUTHOR

I have loved reading since I was a child. I also enjoy baking, photography, and seeing new things. My favorite books are romances with a happily ever after. The world is a crazy place. Sometimes escaping into a great book is the only way I can truly relax. Happily ever after is my favorite type of book, so my stories will end with an HEA, even if the road is a little bumpy getting there. I travel a lot, but currently reside in the Midwest with my family.

Stay up to date with news, book release dates, special promotions and adventures, by visiting my website and social media pages. If you sign up for my newsletter, you will get a free short story! *Christmas with the Nightwood Clan* is a glimpse into the group's first Christmas together and takes place during the Christmas in *A Hairy Situation*.

www.HarperDakota.com
www.HarperDakota.com/Newsletter
Harper's Readers Group

facebook.com/AuthorHarperDakota
instagram.com/harperdakotaauthor

ALSO BY HARPER DAKOTA

Nightwood Clan Series

Bite Me Again

A Hairy Situation

Pointed Love

Forged in Love

* 9 7 9 8 9 8 6 2 5 1 3 7 0 *